Switching Hour

Book 1 , Magic and Mayhem

By

Robyn Peterman

Includes BONUS EXCERPTS
from other books

Acknowledgements

Thank you to so many. Writing may be solitary, but it takes a hell of a lot of people to help finalize the finished product!

Donna McDonald, I would be toast without you. You are my friend, Mystery Science Theatre partner and so much more. Thank you. Rebecca Poole you are a cover guru and I don't want to do a book without you! Mary Yakovets, your editing rocks! My beta readers, Melissa, Jennifer, Christi, Kellie, Amanda and Wanda, you are the BOMB! My Pimpettes are my backbone and I am humbled by your support. My family makes everything worth it and I adore you!

And my readers...I would be nothing without you.

Dedication

For Dakota. You are my sister from another mister. Finding you was one of the loveliest things about this business called writing.

Chapter 1

"If you say or do anything that keeps my ass in the magic pokey, I will zap you bald and give you a cold sore that makes you look like you were born with three lips."

I tried to snatch the scissors from my cell mate's hand, but I might as well have been trying to catch a greased cat.

"Look at my hair," she hissed, holding up her bangs. "They're touching my nose—my fucking *nose*, Zelda. I can't be seen like this when I get out. I swear I'll just do it a little."

"Sandy..." I started.

"It's Sassy," she hissed.

I backed up in case she felt the need to punctuate her correction with a left hook. You can pick your friends, your nose and your bust size, but you can't pick your cell mate in the big house.

"Right. Sorry. Sassy, you have never done anything just a little. What happened the last time you cut your own bangs? Your rap sheet indicates bang cutting is somewhat unhealthy for you."

She winced and mumbled her shame into her collarbone. "That was years ago. Nobody died and that town was a dump to start with."

"Fine." I shrugged. "Cut your bangs. What do I care if you look like a dorkus? We're out of here in an hour. After today we'll never see each other again anyway."

"You know what, Miss High and Mighty?" she shouted, brandishing the shears entirely too close to my head for comfort. "You're in here for murder."

That stopped me dead in my pursuit of saving her from herself. What the hell did I care? Let her cut her bangs up to her hairline and suffer the humiliation of looking five. Maybe I wasn't completely innocent here, but I was no murderer. It was a fucking accident.

"You listen to me, Susie, I didn't murder anyone," I snapped.

"*Sassy.*"

"Whatever." She was giving me a migraine. Swoozie's selective memory was messing with my need to protect her ass. "Oh my Goddess," I yelled. "I didn't sleep with Baba Yaga's boyfriend—you did."

"First of all, we didn't sleep. And how in the hell was I supposed to know Mr. Sexy Pants was her boyfriend?"

"Um, well, let me see... did the fact that he was wearing a *Property of Baba Yaga* t-shirt not ring any fucking bells?"

I was so done. I'd been stuck in a cell with Sassy the Destructive Witch for nine months—sawing my own head off with a butter knife had become a plausible option. I was beyond ready to get the hell out.

"Well, it's not like the Council put you in here just to keep me company. You ran over your own familiar. *On purpose,*" she accused.

I watched in horror as she combed her bangs forward in preparation for blast off and willed myself not to give a rat's ass.

"I did not run over that mangy bastard cat on purpose. The little shit stepped under my wheel."

"Three times?" she inquired politely.

"Yes."

We glared at each other until we were both biting back grins so hard it hurt. As much as I didn't like her, I was grateful to have had a roomie. It would have sucked to serve time alone. And coming up with different female names that started with the letter S had helped pass the time.

"I really need a mirror to do this right," Sassy muttered. She mimed the cutting action by lining up her fingers up on her hair before she commenced.

I walked to the iron bars of our cell and refused to watch. Our tiny living quarters were barren of all modern conveniences, especially those we could perform magic with, like mirrors. We were locked up in Salem, Massachusetts in a hotel from the early 1900s that had been converted to a jail for witches. Our home away from home was cell block D, designated for witches who abused their magic as easily as they changed their underwear.

From the outside the decrepit building was glamoured to look like a charming bed and breakfast, complete with climbing ivy and flowers growing out of every conceivable nook and cranny. Inside it was cold and ugly with barren brick walls covered with Goddess knew what kind of slime. It was warded heavily with magic, keeping all mortals and responsible magic-makers away. At the moment the lovely Sassy and I were the only two inhabitants in the charming hell-hole. Well, us and the humor-free staff of older than dirt witches and warlocks.

I dropped onto my cot and ran my hands through my mass of uncontrollable auburn curls which looked horrid with the orange prison wear. I puckered my full—and sadly lipstick-free-lips as I tried to image myself in the latest Prada. The first damn thing I was going to do when I got out was burn the jumpsuit and buy out Neiman's.

"Fine. We're both here because we messed up, but I still think nine months was harsh for killing a revolting cat and screwing an idiot," I muttered as the ugly reality of my outfit mocked me.

I held my breath and then blew it out as Sassy put the scissors down and changed her mind.

"I can't do this right now. I really need a mirror."

It was the most sane thing she'd uttered in nine months.

"In an hour you'll have one unless you do something stupid," I told her and then froze.

Without warning the magic level ramped up drastically and the stench of centuries-old voodoo drifted to my nose. Sassy latched onto me for purchase and shuddered with terror.

"Do you smell it?" I whispered. I knew her grip would leave marks, but right now that was the least of my problems.

"I do," she murmured back.

"Old lady crouch."

"*What*?" Her eyes grew wide and she bit down on her lip. Hard. "If you make me laugh, I'll smite your sorry ass when we get out. What the hell is old lady crouch?"

My own grin threatened to split my face. My fear of incarceration was clearly outweighed by my need to make crazy Sassy laugh again. "You know—the smell when you go to the bathroom at the country club...powdery old lady crouch."

"Oh my hell, Zelda." She guffawed and lovingly punched me so hard I knew it would leave a bruise. "I won't be able to let that one go."

"Only a lobotomy can erase it." I was proud of myself.

"Well, well, well," a nasally voice cooed from beyond the bars of our cell. "If it isn't the pretty-pretty problem children."

Baba Yaga had to be at least three hundred if she was a day, but witches aged slowly—so she really only looked thirty-fiveish. The more powerful the witch, the slower said witch aged. Baba was powerful, beautiful and had appalling taste in clothes. Dressed right out of the movie *Flash Dance* complete with the ripped sweatshirt, leggings and headband. It was all I could do not to alert the fashion police.

She was surrounded by the rest of her spooky posse, an angry bunch of warlocks who were clearly annoyed to be in attendance.

"Baba Yaga," Sassy said as respectfully as she could without making eye contact.

"Your Crouchness," I muttered and received a quick elbow to the gut from my cellmate.

Baba Yaga leaned against the cell bars, and her torn at the shoulder sweatshirt dripped over her creamy shoulder.

"Zelda and Sassy, you have served your term. Upon release you will have limited magic."

I gasped and Sassy paled. WTF? We'd done our time. *Limited magic?* What did that mean?

"Fuck," I stuttered.

"But... um... Ms. Yaga, that's not fair," Sassy added more eloquently than I had. "We paid our dues. I had to withstand Zelda's company for nine months. I believe that is cruel and unusual punishment."

"Oh my hell," I shouted. "You have got to be kidding me. I fantasized chewing glass, swallowing it and then super gluing my ears shut so I would have to listen to anymore play by plays of *Full House* episodes."

"*Full House* is brilliant and Bob Saget is hot," she grumbled as her face turned red.

"Enough," Baba Yaga hissed as she waved a freshly painted nail at us in admonishment. "You two are on probation, and during that probation you will be strictly forbidden to see each other until you have completed your tasks."

"Not a problem. I don't want to lay eyes on Sujata ever again," I said.

"It's Sassy," she ground out. "And what in the Goddess' name do you mean by *tasks*?"

Baba Yaga smiled—it was not a nice smile.

"Tasks. *Selfless* tasks. And before you two get all uppity with that '*I can't believe you're being so harsh*' drivel, keep in mind that this is a light sentence. Most of the Council wanted you imbeciles stripped of your magic permanently."

That was news. What on earth had I done that would merit that? I conjured up fun things. Sure, they were things I used to my advantage, like shoes and sunny vacations with fruity drinks sporting festive umbrellas in them, served to me on a tropical beach by guys with fine asses...but it wasn't like I took anything from anyone in the process.

"I'm not real clear here," I said warily.

"Oh, I can help with that," Baba Yaga offered kindly. "You, Zelda—how many pairs of Jimmy Choo shoes do you own?"

I mentally counted in my head—kind of. "Um... three?"

Baba Yaga frowned and bright green sparks flew around her head. "Seventy-five and you paid for none of them. Not to mention your wardrobe and cars and the embarrassingly expensive vacations you have taken for free."

When her eyes narrowed dangerously, I swallowed my retort. Plus, I had eighty pairs...

"And you, Sassy, you've used your magic to seduce men and have incurred millions in damages from your temper tantrums. Six buildings and a town. Not to mention your *indiscretion* with my former lover. If I hadn't already been done with him you'd be in solitary confinement for eternity. Can you not see how I had to fight for you?" she demanded, her beautiful eyes fiery.

"Well, when you put it that way," I mumbled.

"There is no other way to put it," she snapped as her mystical lynch mob nodded like the bobble-headed freaks that they were. "Zelda, you have used your magic for self-serving purposes and Sassy, you have a temper that when combined with your magic could be deadly. We are White Witches. We use magic to heal and to make Mother Earth a better place, not to walk the runway and take down cities."

"So what do we have to do?" Sassy asked with a tremor in her voice. She was freaked.

Baba Yaga winked and my stomach dropped to my toes. "There are two envelopes with your tasks in them. You will not share the contents with each other. If you do, you will render yourselves powerless. *Forever.* You have till midnight on All Hallows Eve to complete your assignments and then you will come under review with the Council."

"And if we are unable to fulfill our duty?" I asked, wanting to get all the facts up front.

"You will become mortal."

Shit. My stomach dropped to my toes and I debated between hurling and getting on my knees and begging for mercy. Neither would have done a bit of good...There was no way in hell I could make it in this world as a mortal—I didn't even know how to use a microwave.

And on that alarming and potentially life ending note, Baba Yaga and her entourage disappeared in a cloud of old lady crouch smoke.

"Well, that's fucking craptastic," I said as I warily sniffed my envelope—the one that had appeared out of thin air and landed right between my fingertips.

"You took the words right out of my mouth," Sassy replied as she examined hers.

She tossed her envelope on her cot as though she were afraid to touch it and turned her back on it. I simply shoved mine in the pocket of my heinous orange jumpsuit.

"So that's it? We just do whatever the contents of the envelope tell us to do?" Sassy whined. "Okay, so we're a little self-absorbed, but I do use my magic to heal. Remember when I kind of accidentally punched the guard in the face? I totally healed his nose."

I laughed and rolled my eyes. "He was bleeding all over your one and only pokey jumpsuit."

"Immaterial. I healed him, didn't I?" she insisted.

"And then I zapped your skanky jumpsuit clean," I added, not to be outdone by her list of somewhat dubious selfless acts. "However, I get the feeling that's not the kind of healing magic Baba Yasshole means." I sat down on my own cot, still stunned by our sentence from the Council.

"You know what? Screw Baba Ganoush!" Sassy grunted as she grabbed her envelope and waved it in the air. I sighed and put my hand on her arm to prevent her from doing any damage to her task.

"Yomamma. It's Baba Yomamma, Sassy. And seriously—what choice do we have at this point except to do what she says? You don't want to stay in here, do you? I say we yank up our big girl panties and get this shit done. Deal?"

I stunned myself and Sassy with my responsible reasoning ability.

She made a face but nodded. "Baba Wha-Wha said we couldn't share the contents of our envelopes. There's no way in hell we can open these together and not share."

"Correct. Baba Yosuckmybutt is hateful."

"You want to get turned into a mortal?"

I shuddered. "Fuck no. So now what?" I asked as I played with the offending envelope in my pocket.

"See you on the flip side?" Sassy held up her fist for a bump.

I bumped. "Probably not. While it's been nice in the way a root canal or a canker sore is nice I think it's time for us to part ways."

Sassy grinned and shrugged and I answered with my own.

"So we walk out of here on three?" she asked.

"Yes, we do."

We both took a deep breath. "One, two, three…"

The door of our cell popped open the moment we approached it, clanging and creaking.

We exchanged one last smile before Sassy hung a left and headed down the winding cement path that led to freedom. She made her way down the dimly lit hallway until she was nothing but a small, curvy dot on the horizon.

I clutched the envelope in my pocket with determination and sucked in a huge breath.

And then I hung a right.

Chapter 2

Dearest Zelda,

Apparently your Aunt Hildy died. Violently. You have inherited her home. Go there and make me proud that I didn't strip you of your magic. You will know what to do when you get there.

If you ever use the term "old lady crouch" again while referring to me I will remove your tongue.

xoxo Baba Yaga

P.S. The address is on the back of the note and there is a car for you parked in the garage under the hotel. It's the green one. The purple one is mine. If you even look at it I will put all of your shoes up for sale on eBay. And yes, I am well aware you have eighty pairs.

"Motherhumper, what a bee-otch—put my shoes up for sale, my ass. And who in the hell is Aunt Hildy? I don't have a freakin' aunt named Hildy. Died violently? What exactly does 'died violently' mean?" I muttered to no one as I reread the ridiculous note. Goddess, I wondered what Sassy's note said, but we had gone our separate ways about an hour ago.

My mother was an only child and I hadn't seen her in years—so no Aunt Hildy on that side. My mom, *and I use the term loosely*, was an insanely powerful witch who had met some uber-hot, super weird Vampire ten years ago and they'd gone off to live in a remote castle in Transylvania. The end.

And my father...his identity was anyone's guess. In her day my mother had been a very popular and *active* witch. I suppose Baba *I Know Freakin' Everything* Yaga knew who my elusive daddy was and Hildy must be his sister.

Awesome.

I hustled my ass to the garage and gasped in dismay. In the far corner of the dank, dark, musty-smelling garage sat a car... a green car. A lime green car. Even better, it was a lime green Kia. Was Baba YoMamma fucking joking? Why did I have to drive anywhere? I was a witch. I could use magic to get wherever I wanted to go.

Crap.

Did I even have enough magic to transport? Could I end up wedged in a time warp and stuck for eternity?

And what, pray tell, was this? A Porsche? Baba Yoyeastinfection drove a Porsche... of course she did.

I eyed the purple Porsche with envy and for a brief moment considered keying it. The look on Boobie Yoogie's face would be worth it. Another couple of years in the magic pokey plus having to watch my fancy footwear be auctioned off on eBay was enough to curb my impulse. However, I did lick my finger and smear it on the driver's side mirror. I was told not to look at it. The cryptic note mentioned nothing about touching it.

Glancing down at my orange jumpsuit I cringed. Did they really expect me to wear this? What the hell had become of me? I was a thirty-year-old paroled witch in orange prison wear and tennis shoes. My fingers ached to clothe myself in something cute and sexy. Did I dare? How would they even know?

Wait... she knew I called her old lady crouch. She would certainly know if I magicked up some designer duds. Shitballs. Orange outfit and red hair it was.

Thankfully the car had a GPS, not that I knew how to work anything electronic. I was a witch, for god's sake. I normally flicked my fingers, chanted a spell or wiggled my nose. The address of my inheritance was in West Virginia. How freakin' far was West Virginia from Salem, Massachusetts?

Apparently eleven hours and twenty-one minutes.

It took me exactly forty-five minutes of swearing and punching the dashboard to figure that little nugget out. Bitchy Vicky was officially my least favorite person in the world. However, I was a little proud to have made the damn GPS work without using magic or blowing the car up.

***

Five hours into the trip I was itchy, bloated and had a massive stomachache. Beef jerky and Milk Duds were not my friend. Top that off with a corn dog and two sixty-four ounce caffeinated sodas and I was a clusterfuck waiting to happen.

Thank the Goddess New England was gorgeous in the fall. The colors were breathtaking, but they did little to calm my indigestion. The Kia had no radio reception, but luckily it did come with a country compilation CD that was stuck in the CD player. I was going deaf from the heartfelt warblings about pickup trucks, back roads and barefoot rednecks.

Pretending to be mortal sucked. Six more hours and twenty-one minutes to go—shit. Sadly I found myself longing for even the hideous company of Sassy. Being alone was getting old.

"I can do this. I have to do this. I will do this," I shouted at the alarmed driver of a minivan while stopped at a traffic light in Bumfuck, Idon'tknowwhere.

"I'm baaaaaaack," something hissed from behind me.

"What the fu... ?" I shrieked and jerked the wheel to the right, avoiding a bus stop and landing the piece of crap car in a shallow ditch. "Who said that?"

"I diiiiiiiid," the ominous voice whispered. "Have yooooooou misssssssed me?"

"Um, sure," I mumbled as I quietly removed my seatbelt and prepared to dive out of the car. Maybe I could catch a lift with the woman I'd terrified in the minivan. "I've missed you a ton."

"You look like shiiiiiit in ooooorrrrangeeeee," it informed me.

That stopped me. Whatever monster or demon was in the backseat had just gone one step too far.

Scare me? Fine.

Insult me? Fry.

"Excuse me?" I snapped and whipped around to smite the fucker. Where was he? Was he invisible? "Show yourself."

"Down heeeeere on the floooooor," the thing said.

Peering over the seat, I gagged and threw up in my mouth just a little. This could not be happening. I pinched myself hard and yelped from the pain. It *was* happening and it was probably going to get ugly in about twelve seconds.

"Um, hi Fabio, long time no see," I choked out, wondering if I made a run for it if he would follow and kill me. Or at the very least, would he get behind the wheel of the Kia and run me over... three times. "You're looking kind of alive."

"Thank youuuuuuuuu," he said as he hopped over the seat and landed with a squishy thud entirely too close to me.

I plastered myself against the door and debated my next move. Fabio looked bad. He still resembled a cat, but he was kind of flat in the middle, his head was an odd shape and his tail cranked to the left. Most of his black fur still covered him except for a large patch on his face, which made him resemble a pinkish troll. He didn't seem too angry, but I did kill him. To be fair, I didn't mean to. I didn't know he was under the wheel and I kind of freaked and hit reverse and drive several times before I got out and screamed bloody murder.

"So what are you doing here?" I inquired casually, careful not to make eye contact.

"Not exxxxxxactly sure." He shook his little black semi-furred head and an ear fell off.

"Oh shit," I muttered and flicked it to the floor before he noticed. "I'm really sorry about killing you."

"No worrrrrrries. I quite enjoyed being buried in a Prrrrraaada shoeeee box."

"I thought that was a nice touch," I agreed. "Did you notice I left the shoe bags in there as a blanket and pillow?"

"Yesssssssssssss. Very comfortable." He nodded and gave me a grin that made my stomach lurch.

"Alrighty then, the question of the hour is are you still dead... or um..."

"I thiiiink I'm aliiiiive. As soon as I realliiiized I was breathing I loooooked for you."

"Wow." I was usually more eloquent, but nothing else came to mind.

"I have miiiiiiiisssed you, Zeeeeldaaaa."

Great, now I felt horrible. I killed him and he rose from the dead to find me because he missed me. I should take him in my arms and cuddle him, but I feared all the jerky and Duds would fly from my mouth if I tried. He deserved far better than me.

"Look, Fabio... I was a shitty witch for you. You should find a witch that will treat you right."

"But I loooooooovvve you," he said quietly. His little one-eared head drooped and he began to sniffle pathetically.

"You shouldn't love me," I reasoned. "I'm selfish and I killed you—albeit accidentally—and I'm wearing orange."

"I can fix that," he offered meekly. "Would that make you loooooooove meeeee?"

I felt nauseous and it wasn't from all the crap I'd shoved in my mouth while driving to meet my destiny. The little disgusting piece of fur had feelings for me. Feelings I didn't even come close to deserving or returning. And now to make matters worse, he was offering to magic me some clothes. If I said yes, it was a win-win. I'd get new clothes and he'd think I loved him. Asshats on fire, what in the hell was love anyway?

"Um...I would seem kind of shallow if I traded my love for clothes," I mumbled as I bit down on the inside of my cheek to keep from declaring my worthless love in exchange for non-orange attire.

"Well, youuuuuu are somewhat superficial, but that's not alllllllll your fault," Fabio said as he squished a little closer and placed the furry side of his head in my lap.

"Thank you, I think."

A compliment was a compliment, no matter how insulting.

"You're most welcome," he purred. "How would you know what loooooove is? Your mother was a hoooooooker and your poor father was in the darrrrrk about your existence most of your liiiiiiiife."

"My mother was loose," I admitted, "but she did the best she could. However, my father, whoever the motherfuck he is, just took off after he knocked up my mom. And P.S.—I'm the only one allowed to call my mom a hooker. As nice as the fable was you told me about my dad... it's bullshit."

"Nooooooooo, actually it's not," Fabio said as he lifted his piercing green eyes to mine.

"Do you know the bastard?" I demanded, noticing for the first time how our eyes matched. That wasn't uncommon. Most familiars took on the traits of their witches, but I wished he hadn't taken on mine. It would make it much harder to pawn the thing off on someone else if he looked too much like me.

"I knoooooow of him."

"So where the hell is he if he knows about me now?" My eyes narrowed dangerously and blue sparks began to cover my arms.

Fabio quickly backed away in fear of getting crispy. "Assssssssssss the story goes, a spell was cast on him by your mooooooother when he learned of your existence. From what I've heard he's been trying to break the spellllllllll by doing penance."

I rolled my eyes and laughed. "How's that working out for the assmonkey?"

18

"Apparently not veeeeeeery well if he hasn't shown himself yet."

I considered Fabio's fairytale and wished for a brief moment it was true. Maybe my father didn't know about me. I always thought he didn't want me. That's what my mom had said. Of course she was certifiable and I'd left her house the moment I'd turned eighteen. I did love her but only in the same way a dog still loves the owner who kicks it.

Fabio's story was utter crap, but it was sweet that he cared. Other than Baba Yopaininmyass, not many did.

"Where did you learn all that fiction?" I asked as I eased the lime green piece of dog poo back onto the road before the police showed up and mistook me for an escaped convict.

"Yourrrrrrrr file," he answered as he dug his claws into the strap of the seat belt and pulled it across his mangled body. "Evvvvvvery familiar gets a file on their witch."

"Here, let me," I said as I pulled the strap and clicked it into the lock. "Was there anything else interesting in my file?"

The damn cat knew more about me than I did.

"Nothing I caaaaaan share."

I pursed my lips so I wouldn't swear at him—hard but doable. I wanted info and I knew how to get it. "What if I reattached your ear? Would you tell me one thing you're not supposed to?" I bargained.

"I'mmmmm missssssssing an ear?" he shrieked, aghast.

"Yep, I flicked it under the seat so you wouldn't flip out."

His breathing became erratic. I worried he would heave a hairball or something worse. "Yesssssss, reattach it, please."

I opened my senses, and let whatever magic Baba Yasshole had let me keep flow through me. Light purple healing flames covered my arms, neck and face. Fabio's ear floated up from under the passenger seat and drifted to his

19

head. As it connected back, I had a thought. It was selfish... and not.

"Hey Fab, do you mind if I fill in the fur on your face?" It would be so much easier to look at the little bastard if I didn't see raw cat skin.

"Ohhhhhhhhhh my, I'm missing fur?" He was positively despondent. Clearly he hadn't looked in a mirror since his resurrection.

"Um, it's just a little," I lied. "I can fix it up in a jiff."

"Thhhhhhank you, that would be loooovely."

The magic swirled through me. It felt so good. The pokey had blocked me from using magic and I'd missed it terribly. The silky warm purple mist skimmed over Fabio's body and the hair reappeared. Without his permission I unflattened his midsection, reshaped his head and uncranked his tail. It was the least I could do since I'd caused it in the first place.

"There. All better," I told him and glanced over to admire my handiwork. He looked a lot less mangled. He was still a bit mangy, but that was how he'd always been. At least he no longer looked like living road kill. "Your turn."

"Your Aunt Hildy was your father's sissssssster and she wasssss freakin' crazy," he hissed with disgust.

"You knew her?"

"Ahh no, but sheeeeeee was legendary," he explained.

"Why the hell did she leave me her house?" I asked, hoping for some more info. I'd already assumed she was my deadbeat dad's sister. I wanted something new.

"I suppose you will take ooooover for her," Fabio informed me as he lifted and extended his leg so he could lick his balls.

"Get your mouth off your crotch while we're having a conversation," I snapped.

"Youuuuu would do it if youuuuuuu could," he said.

"Probably," I muttered as I zoomed past six cars driving too slow for my mood. "But since I can't, you're not allowed to either."

"Can I dooooooo it in private?" he asked.

"Um, sure. Now tell me what crazy old Aunt Hildy did for a living so I know what I'm getting into here."

"No clue," Fabio said far too quickly.

"You know, I could run your feline ass over again," I threatened.

"Yeeeeeep, but I have six lives left."

I put my attention back on the road. "Great. That's just great."

Chapter 3

"What the fu... ? *Fabio, I'm naked*," I screamed somewhere around mile marker thirtytwowhatthehell in Pennsylvania. "What are you doing?"

"Trying to give youuuu a new outfiiiiit," Fabio whined as he turned away in horror.

I was unsure if I was more pissed that I was naked in the driver's seat of a lime green Kia or about the fact that he clearly found me heinous to look at.

"You know," I ground out through clenched teeth, "most people consider me hot."

"Yessssssss, well, I'm a cat and I find yoooooour nudity allllaaaarming."

"Then dress me," I snapped. "In something really cute and expensive to make up for insulting my exposed knockers."

"Your knockers are loooooovely, but it's not apppppppropriate for me to ogle your undraaaaaped body."

He was a freakin' wreck.

"Is that against some kind of witch slash familiar law?" I demanded as I looked down at myself. I looked good. Witches had crazy fast metabolisms and all of us were stupidly pretty.

"Yesssssssss," he said as he twitched uncomfortably in his seat.

"Naked here," I reminded him.

The car filled with magic so quickly I gasped and held on to the steering wheel with all my might. The little fucker was strong. Who knew he had so much magic stored up in his mangy little carcass? A heat covered my body and I swerved to miss a semi truck.

"For the love of the Goddess," I shouted. "Hurry up or we're going to die here."

"Do youuuu want paaaaants or a skirt?" he asked.

"At the moment I'm not picky. I'm panicked. Just make sure it's not orange and I'll be happy."

"Assssss youuuu wish."

The magic receded as quickly as it had begun. I was too shaken to even look down to see if I was dressed. I was getting rid of him as soon as I could. He was a fucking menace—not that I was a prize—but an imbalanced cat was more insanity than even I could handle.

"Dooooo you liiiike it?" he asked with an absurd amount of pride in his voice.

"I'll tell you in an hour when I get up the courage to look down. Where in the hell did you get so much magic? Familiars are not supposed to be stronger than their witches."

"I'm nooooot stronger," he insisted. "Youuuuu are stronger thaaaaaan you know."

"Well, at the moment I'm not. Boobah Yumpa has me running on half a tank," I told him. "It's part of my punishment for killing you."

"Buuuuut I'm not deeeeead," he replied logically.

He was correct, but Butthole Yaga never changed her mind. Ever. It was actually something I liked about her, though I would never tell her. I'd grown up so horrendously, any female authority figure who had semi-sane rules was appealing to me.

"Yeah, she doesn't cave easily."

"You're wearing Maaaaax Midnight jeans and a vintage Minnie Mouuuuuse t-shirt with hot piiiink combat boots," he said.

That gave me pause. Hot pink combat boots were beyond awesome and Max Midnight jeans cost seven hundred dollars a pop. My freakin' cat had good taste. Maybe I'd keep him a little while longer.

"Are you serious?"

"Yessssss. I can change you iiiiif that diiispleases you."

"NO," I shouted. I wasn't sure if we would live through another change, plus if what he said was true I was a very happy camper. I glanced down and sighed with joy and relief. He was true to his word. I looked hot. "I like it."

His purr was cute until I looked over at him and noticed he was going for his nut sack again. "What did I tell you about that?" I glared at him in disgust.

"Soooooorrry," he whispered contritely. "Habit."

"Well, Fabio, you're going to have to break that one or I'll get you neutered."

"Youuuuuuu wouldn't." He gasped and crossed his little kitty legs over his jewels.

"Try me."

That shut him up for about five minutes and seven seconds.

"Are weeeeeeee there yet?"

"No."

"How much loooooooonger?"

"I don't know."

"More thaaaaaan two hours?"

"No clue."

"More than three hoooooouuuuuurs?"

I bit down on my bottom lip so I didn't shout a spell at him that would permanently destroy his voice box. I was certain it wouldn't go over well with Booboo Yoogu.

"Willlllllll it be soooooon?"

"Fabio?"

"Yesssssss, Zelda?"

"Lick your balls."

"Realllllllllly?" He was so excited I cringed.

"Yes really, but get in the back seat. However, if I hear any slurping or purring I will throw your furry ass out of the window and leave you there. Are we clear?"

"Duuuuuly noted."

He jumped in the back seat and we had a peaceful ride the rest of the way there.

***

Aunt Hildy's house sat high on a hill and was the most beautiful thing I'd ever seen. It was a white Victorian with a wraparound porch and turrets. Wildflowers covered the grounds and the trees blazed with color. Only a few major drawbacks kept me from screaming with joy at my good fortune.

For one, it was located in the middle of nowhere. Since we had little to no supplies we trekked to town. The closest town, if you could call it that, was a half an hour away and consisted of Main Street. The town square was dominated by a statue of a cement bear missing one side of his head. The rest of the block included a barbershop, hardware store, gas station and a mom and pop grocery. Awesome—not.

We made a quick stop at the gas station. I gassed up the Kia with a credit card, *probably stolen,* that Fabio happened to have and then went into the grocery. I winced at the rotting fruit and vegetables as I headed for the frozen and canned aisles. Ten frozen pizzas, two tubs of ice cream, and fifteen cans of brand-less spaghetti later, I got in line at the checkout behind the hottest guy I'd ever seen.

What in the hell was the Goddess's gift to women doing in Buttcrack, West Virginia? Maybe this place wasn't so bad. His ass in his jeans was enough to make my mouth water and he smelled like heaven.

Nine months in the magic pokey were enough to make any girl horny, but this guy was something else. I made a couple of girly sounds hoping to get his attention, but failed—so I touched his butt. Not grabbed—kind of brush-touched accidently on purpose.

"You could have asked first," a deep sexy voice informed me without even turning around.

"I'm sorry," I said politely to his back. "I have no idea what you're talking about."

"You could have requested to cop a feel of my ass." He turned around and I almost dropped to the floor. He wasn't just pretty, he was redonkulous gorgeous. Dark wavy hair, blue eyes, lashes that belonged on a girl, a body to die for and a face that would make the Angels weep. Oh. My. Hell.

"It was in my way. Consider yourself lucky. I almost slapped it."

His laugh went all the way to my woowoo. I nearly crushed the can of Spaghettios I was clutching.

"Well, beautiful girl," he drawled in a Southern accent that made my brain short out, "I'd suggest you watch your ass. If it gets in my way I'll do much more than slap it."

"Promise?" I challenged.

He considered me for a long moment and then winked. "Promise."

I held on to the counter as I watched him walk out of the store and realized I didn't even know his name. Whatever. I didn't need to get into any messy relationship. Hell, I'd never maintained a relationship in my life. I'd always had lots of boyfriends, but the minute it got serious I was out of there. Fast. Plus, I rarely dated mortals. Mr. Fine Ass didn't really look like relationship material. However, he did look like awesome one or two or three night stand material... Crap. I supposed I'd have to grocery shop on a regular basis. I grabbed my bags and went back to my new reality.

"Diiiiid you get my pasta?" Fabio inquired. He'd moved back to the front seat as he was clearly done attending to his gonads.

"Yep."

"Annnnd fresh tomatoes, baaaaasil and garlic?"

"Yep." He'd find out soon enough he was going to be eating Spaghettios. That was the price he'd have to pay for cleaning his Johnson for three hours, plus the fresh stuff would have killed him more certainly than my car had. "You ready to check out our new digs?"

"Asssss ready as I'll ever beeeeeee," he said with disgust.

"I'm not really buying that you didn't know Hildy," I said dryly. "You seem to be having an awful lot of issues here."

"It's heeeeer reputation," he shot back. "I don't liiiike this."

"Well buddy, neither do I, but if I don't figure out why I'm here Buttcrack Yoogiemamma will turn me into a mortal on Halloween. So we're going to the house and we are going to fucking like it. You got it?"

"Yesssssss," he answered morosely. "Gotttt it."

Chapter 4

"Oh my Goddess," I screeched. "What's not to like?"

The house was as beautiful on the inside as it was on the outside. Overstuffed comfy furniture and Persian rugs covered shiny hardwood floors. Windows stretched from the floor to the ceiling and the house was bathed with autumn sunshine. The ornate crown molding was divine and the stone fireplace was to die for. The kitchen table was a distressed oak and seated at least twelve. The appliances were top of the line and there was a fully stocked wine fridge. Aunt Hildy was all right in my book.

Upstairs consisted of seven bedrooms, all with king-sized beds and gorgeous down quilts. The colors were calming and comfortable. However, foremost in my mind was how she died. That thought did not calm me.

"Hey Fabio, I'm coming back downstairs. If you're licking your sack you better stop now," I warned. I thought it was very kind of me to give him a heads up. He was lounging on the sofa looking very guilty.

"Hiiiiiiiii," he said with an embarrassed chuckle.

I decided to ignore his obsession with his dangly bits and move on to more important matters. "Do you have any idea how Aunt Hildy died?"

He sat silently and stared.

"Do you like your testes?" I asked politely.

"Yesssssss."

"Then start talking, feline."

"It is unknoooooown, but her body is missing," he replied warily.

"You know this from my file?" I inquired.

"Posssssssibly."

"Um, she was a witch I assume…"

"Don't assssssume. Makes an assssss out of youuuu and meeeeee."

"Oh my Goddess," I bellowed and accidently set a table on fire with my fury. "Was she a witch or not?" I quickly chanted a water spell to put out the flames before I burned my new house down.

"Yesssssss."

Now we were getting somewhere. "Did she break Council laws?"

"Not as far as I knooooow. I have told you alllllll that was in the fiiiile."

I wasn't sure I believed him, but it would do for now. "I wonder where her body is."

"In Helllllll?"

"All right," I yelled. "Give it up, you little shit. You knew her. Didn't you?"

"Fiiiiine. Yes, I kneeeeeew her, but I haven't secceen her in years."

"How many?" I demanded.

"A huuuundred or so."

That shut me up. I had no freakin' clue cats lived so long. "How old are you?"

"Two hundred and threeeeeeeeeee."

"Were you her familiar?"

"Noooooooooooooooo, absolutely not," he huffed indignantly.

"So you do know what her job was." I approached him and he backed away. Blue and pink flames whipped up my arms. I was pissed. He was *my* damn cat and he was supposed to let me know what was what. "Spit it out."

"Gooooo to the basement. Youuuuuu will see."

"There's a basement?"

"There's aaaaaaa baaaasement."

***

There was definitely a basement and it was creepy. It was all cement cinderblock and lined with huge empty dog kennels. Did she raise Saint Bernards? I mean, what the hell? A family of four could have lived in each of the cages. There had to be at least twenty.

A large rectangular metal table sat in the middle of the room and was stacked high with clean blankets and pillows. An array of clothing in every size imaginable was in labeled bins beneath the long table. Toiletries filled several more bins. One kennel was filled with winter coats, hats, gloves, and boots.

Confusion didn't even begin to cover what was running through my brain. Did she keep prisoners down here? Was she a mad scientist who experimented on humans and then dressed them warmly and sent them on their way?

I glanced around and looked for instruments of torture, but only found a couple of first aid kits. The pieces did not fit and I had no clue what this room was for. The cat was going to talk or he was going to lose his 'nads.

Of course the cat was gone. I was going to kill him so dead when I found him. How was I supposed to figure out what I was supposed to do? There was no way I was going to let Bushy Yuba turn me mortal on Halloween.

A note—maybe Aunt Hildy had left me a note with instructions on it.

I ransacked the entire house for two hours and came up empty-handed. However, I did discover Aunt Hildy was anally organized and wore a size six. That kind of sucked because I was a four and she had some expensive shit. She did have a bizarre collection of tote bags. I grinned as I went through them, my favorite had to be the one reading *You Only Get Out What You Put Into It*. Weird.

Depressed and no closer to knowing anything, I dropped down on the smooshy couch and cried. At least I was wearing awesome clothes. I didn't think I could take it if I was still clad in orange. Glancing around through my tears, I realized Aunt Hildy didn't have a TV or even a radio. I was tempted to wiggle my nose and conjure up a massive flat screen, but that would be using magic for my own gain. I was fairly sure that was a big no-no.

Exhausted from the drive and pissed at Fabio, I laid back on the couch and closed my eyes. I'd eat later. I needed to sleep. When my head was clear I'd kill the cat and figure out the mystery. However, sleep was impossible with all the racket the damn cat was making on the front porch. How did something so small sound like a herd of elephants?

I stomped to the porch, ready to let him have it. "Fabio, what the hell are you…"

Holy crap on a stick, it wasn't Fabio at all. The porch was crowded with animals. Injured animals—bleeding, injured animals. WTF? They all looked at me with fear in their eyes and my stomach sunk to my toes. Shit, was Hildy a wild animal vet? I didn't really like animals that much. I'd even killed my cat. I couldn't take care of a bunch of smelly, bleeding animals.

"Go. Go home," I ordered. "Aunt Hildy died and you guys stink. I have a very active gag reflex and this isn't working for me."

They looked at me like I had three heads and not one of them moved an inch. Son of a bitch. Fairly sure they weren't going to eat me, I slumped down on the steps and dropped my head into my hands. A little wet nose nudged me and gently licked my face. The breath was horrid, but the gesture was sweet. He was a small baby raccoon with huge brown eyes and he was cute.

"Hi," I whispered and scratched his head. He made little chattering noises and my stupid heart melted. "You guys should go. I have no clue what you want or need."

I looked around to see all the other guests. There was a mother raccoon, a bear, a deer, a beaver and a skunk. I jumped up and backed away. There was no way I was going to get sprayed. I only had one set of clothing unless Fabio showed his bastard ass back up and I was not going to smell like skunk ass. Period.

"If you blow your stinker off, I will fry you where you stand. Do you understand me?"

The skunk nodded his little head and I almost passed out. Did the little stinkbomb maker understand me? Was that even possible? Was it because I was a witch? I'd never heard of that before, but what the hell did I know? I'd skipped most of my classes in magic school. I was too busy shopping and partying. Damn it, bad move on my part.

"Look, guys," I said as I walked back to the front door. "I can't help you. You smell bad and you're animals. I have to figure out how my aunt died and probably who killed her. You dudes have to go."

The tiny raccoon chattered and scampered around my feet. Blood dripped from a wound on the back of his head. What had happened to these animals?

"Shit," I muttered. "All right... all you fuckers get in a straight line and I'll fix you a little."

They quickly formed a line, further evidence they could understand me. This of course freaked me out so I decided to ignore it.

Sucking in a cleansing breath I let the magic take me. Again, as it happened earlier with Fabio the nut licker, purple flames engulfed my upper body. I giggled as they tickled my nose. I wanted to hold on to the flames and bask in them, but there were a bunch of odoriferous wounded furry things staring at me with wonder.

Shit. Being good sucked.

Grudgingly, I let go and let the purple mist bathe the hairy bodies of my visitors. The sighs, chattering, yips and happy growls actually made me feel kind of nice, but not nice enough to hang out with the zoo on my porch.

"Okay, outta here. I did my thing—now you have to go," I told them as I walked into the house.

I didn't look back. If that damn little raccoon made eye contact I was liable to invite them all in and that was so not happening.

"Have a good life," I muttered as I shut the door firmly behind me and locked it.

I was tired and hungry. I had also depleted myself magically. For not having used magic in nine months, I'd just used a ton fixing the hairball brigade. All I wanted to do was fall asleep in front of the TV watching *Project*

Runway but I couldn't even do that. How in the hell did someone live in this day and age without a damn TV?

I skipped eating, climbed the stairs and threw myself down on the first bed I came to. Tomorrow would be a new day. I could figure out what I was to do and if Fabio came back, maybe I could trick him into conjuring up a TV.

I smiled as I snuggled into the fluffy comforter.

I'd solve all the world's problems tomorrow.

Chapter 5

Bright morning sunlight poured through the window and singed my half-shut eyeballs. I rolled over with a grumpy moan only to come face-to-balls with Fabio.

"Is there a reason your scrotum is in my face?" I spat as I sat up quickly and moved to the other side of the bed.

"Gooooood morning to youuuuu too," Fabio said as he stretched his skinny kitty frame.

"It's not a good morning and where the hell did you go last night?"

"I had a feeew errands to run and theeen I wasssss checking the area for femaaaale cats," he informed me.

"And did you find any?" I asked, even though it was a question I had no desire to have answered.

"Niiiiine." He was positively giddy and I was positively nauseous.

All the things I considered saying were so foul and rude, I actually held my tongue for a full ten seconds.

"Well, I hope you used protection. The last thing we need is a bunch of little ball-licking Fabios running around," I muttered.

I rolled out of bed and landed in a pile of the most fabulous clothes and shoes I'd ever seen.

"Oh my Goddess," I squealed. "Are these for me?"

"Do youuuuu liiike?" he asked excitedly.

"Oh my hell, I love!"

There had to be at least six pairs of low rise Max Midnight jeans and a Max mini skirt. Loads of camisoles, sheer tops, vintage t-shirts and gorgeous cashmere sweaters with the price tags still on them exploded out of designer bags.

And the shoes... platform Pradas and kick ass motorcycle boots. I was in heaven. Not to mention the cat hadn't skimped on the undergarments either. Fleur of England panties, thongs and bras in every color imaginable. If the feline kept this up I might end up loving him after all. Shallow? Yes, but at the moment I didn't care.

"You did this for me?"

"I want you to be haaaappy, and you are sooooo pretttty you deserve loooovely things," he said quietly.

His words hit me hard. I sat back and stared with dismay at the beautiful clothes.

"I don't deserve any of this. You seem to have forgotten I smooshed you with a car. I've been shitty to you while you insist on being nice. It makes me feel horrid."

I fingered a camel-colored cashmere sweater longingly, but I knew what I had to do. I dropped my head between my knees and gulped in air so I didn't puke. Doing the right thing sucked ass. Big time.

"Take them all back. I'll just wear the clothes I have on," I gasped out in pain.

"Noooo can doooo," Fabio said as he whipped up a little magic and all the price tags disappeared from the garments. "The taaags are gone and I peeeeed on the receipt. Smeeeellls awful. You willl have to keep these things or I will get arrrrrrrrrested."

"Did you steal them?" I asked, watching him closely.

"Not exxxactly," he hedged. "I'm juuust unsure if the credit card I used was cooompletely legal."

"Wait." I shook my head and tried to figure this out. "Did you go to a store as a cat and buy this stuff?"

"Um, no. I speeellled a woman in Paris and she bought them for meeeeee," he explained as if it was the most logical thing in the world.

ROBYN PETERMAN

"You went to freakin' Paris last night? How in the hell did you get to Paris and back? Not to mention the little fact you defiled nine cats in eight hours?"

He was so full of shit.

"I transsssported."

"Familiars can't transport without their witches." I raised my eyebrows and waited for his next line of crap.

"I caaaaaaan."

I narrowed my eyes and stared him down. What kind of familiar was he? Was he even a familiar at all?

Did he gain super powers when he came back from the dead?

Was he a spy for Bundtcake Yaga?

Should I pursue this line of thinking or did I enjoy my windfall?

Goddess, decisions were hard. I sucked in another huge breath and made my choice. I was absolutely positive it was the wrong choice, but I decided to stand by it.

"Because I don't want you to get arrested I will keep the clothes. I'd like to go on record and say I don't buy your story, but I will be bitchier than normal if I have to wear the same outfit for a month. So again, I am keeping the clothes for your safety."

"Woooonderful," he purred and rubbed his stubbly little head along my arm. "Gooooo and shower. I will whiiiiip up some breakfaaast."

"Ooookay," I said as I grabbed some barely-there undies, jeans and a t-shirt and made my way to the bathroom. He was going to have limited supplies considering all we had was ice cream, frozen pizza and canned spaghetti. "Good luck with that."

***

"Hey Fabio, I am lookin' good today," I sang as I ran down the stairs in my new fabu ensemble. I still felt a little bad about keeping the clothes, but one glance in the mirror and I shoved that guilt to the compartment in my head I called "denial".

The smell of bacon and eggs wafted from the kitchen. Craptastic, did he rob a grocery store too? We were going to have to talk. Magic was one thing, but bad credit cards were another.

"Cooooome and eattttttttt," he yelled from the kitchen.

We'd talk later. My stomach was empty and my mouth was watering.

"Dude, I..." I stopped short and stared in shock. Seated around the table and eating off of china were my zoo friends. WTF? The skunk, bear, deer, beaver, mamma raccoon and baby raccoon all slurped happily from plates. This was so not happening.

"Um...no. This is not good. Animals do not sit at the table and eat bacon and eggs."

"And paaaancakes," Fabio added.

"Not helping, cat. We'll discuss where you got the ingredients later," I snapped as I tried to pull the bear out of his chair. I wondered briefly if Fabio had gone back to the grocery and if Hot Ass Guy had been there. No time to think about sex when I had a fuzzy menagerie in my kitchen. The damn bear had to weigh five hundred pounds and was going nowhere fast.

What was I thinking? And why wasn't I afraid of these intruders?

They all started yipping at once. I pinched the bridge of my nose and exhaled a loud breath. My body started to glow. I knew I was seconds away from incinerating the house. Worst of all, I was almost positive I was hearing actual words amidst the noise.

"Enough," I shouted and sat down next to the bear. "You guys are supposed to live in the fucking wild," I explained. "Not in my house."

I noticed I'd missed a few wounds on the bear and beaver. Maybe if I fixed them all up they would go.

"You're noooot being veeery hospitable," Fabio chastised me.

I groaned and banged my head on the table. "Okay, here's the deal. Finish your breakfast and then I'll do a little voodoo on your wounds and then you'll leave. And if any of you even chip a piece of china I will shove it up your ass. Understood?"

They all nodded happily and went back to their meals. Fucked up had just become my new normal.

"Uh ohhhhhh, I smell old laaaaady crouch," Fabio hissed.

"What?" I choked out as a large piece of pancake lodged in my throat. "You know what old lady crouch is?"

"Doesn't everyoooone?" he asked.

He was definitely my cat.

"Is it here?" I sniffed the air as I stood and started yanking animals from their chairs.

"Incooooooming. I'd say about ten minutes till shooowdown."

"Shit," I shouted. "You dudes need to skedaddle."

"Zeeeelda, they're injured. Weeee can't put them out," the damn cat reasoned.

He was correct and I was an ass. I had no clue why, but I didn't want Baba Yogo and her entourage to see a National Geographic show in Aunt Hildy's kitchen. They already thought I was partially unhinged. This would prove it. "You all will hide in the…"

"Baaaasement?" Fabio volunteered.

"Yes, the basement. Follow me."

Hustling the zoo to the basement took approximately three minutes. The bastards could move and they seemed to know their way. They all grabbed blankets and pillows and went to cages.

"Um, you guys don't have to get into those things. You can just hang out and you know, play or something. Quietly," I added.

They either didn't understand, which I found hard to believe, or they were just ignoring me. Whatever. If they wanted to sleep in the kennels who was I to complain? Everyone laid down and snuggled into their blankets except the bear—who squatted.

No freakin' way. I marched over to his cage and got up in his face. "This is not the woods and you are not going to take a shit. Do you understand me?"

He shrugged, grunted and flopped onto his back. If he took a dump he was going to eat it. Period.

"I'll be back as soon as I get rid of Baba Yomamma and her warlock buddies. Stay here and don't make noise."

I ran back to the kitchen to clean up the evidence of the breakfast, but Fabio was two steps ahead of me. He'd cleaned the kitchen and was now cleaning his nuts. I looked away and let him have at it. He did warn me so I supposed he deserved a little cleansing time.

"Hello, Zelda," Baba Yaga purred as she and her idiot cronies appeared in a cloud of crouch smoke.

"Baba Yaga," I muttered and gave her a quick hug. She was sporting a sparkly green spandex body suit and a blue sequined headband. Someday I was going to have to do a style intervention, but today was not that day. Her eyes roved over me and my stomach clenched in terror. Crap, I was wearing designer duds. "I didn't do it," I shouted frantically. "Fabio thought I looked shitty in orange, *which I do*, and he wanted me to have something decent to wear so he went to Paris and…"

"Your familiar went to Paris without you?" a little crinkly warlock demanded in a nasty tone. "Impossible."

"He did," I insisted. I was not going back to jail for a crime I didn't commit. "I'm guessing since he rose from the dead, he's developed wondrous, mindboggling, kick ass super powers."

Everyone looked over at my cat who was getting down on his balls.

"And clearly a need for squeaky-clean genitals," I mumbled as the entourage gaped in disgust.

Fabio, uncaring that his grooming was being watched, looked up, yawned and coughed up a mother of a hairball. I couldn't have been prouder if he was my own child. The gasps and appalled huffs were music to my ears. I knew Baba and her bunch weren't long for my house. My cat was awesome.

"Well, Zelda, he's quite a charmer," Baba Yaga noted dryly. She tossed her hair, which she'd had cut into a heinous mullet right out of the 80's as she wandered the room and examined the knickknacks. "Have you noticed anything unusual here?"

"Um… define unusual."

She eyed me critically and then gently began to pet a very happy Fabio. "You tell me. Anything odd? Ghosts? Attacks? Waves of strange magic? Fairies or Vampires? Love?"

"No. Nothing like that," I answered, relieved. Crap, was that what was coming? And how exactly did love fit into that fucked-up mix? "Is that what my mission involves?"

"I certainly hope not," she said as she rounded up the arrogant warlocks to make her always dramatic exit. "You seem to be doing well. I shall leave you to your duties."

"Wait," I shouted. Everyone froze and tense magic swirled through the room. Yelling at three-hundred-year-old witches and warlocks clearly wasn't the norm. "Do you want to give me any hints?"

Baba Yaga approached me and I shrank a little. What kind of idiot was I? Baba Yogicrazy could turn me into a goo pile with a flick of her pinkie. She placed her manicured hand on my face and looked me right in the eye. "You will be fine, Zelda. I believe in you."

With that she puffed away and left me more confused than ever. She believed in me? She was smoking crack. No one believed in me. Not even me.

"Sheeeeee is an odd oooone," Fabio volunteered.

"What was that about?" I asked. "That visit was totally random. I still don't know what the hell I'm supposed to do. If I get turned back into a mortal because no one gave me a direction sheet I will be..."

"Aaangry?"

"Worse," I said as I searched for the appropriate word.

"Pissssssed?" Fabio guessed.

"Closer," I muttered. "But not quite strong enough."

"Fuuuuucking furious enough tooooo take the wooorld by its ballllls and twist until it screeeeamms uncle or explooodes?"

I was speechless for seven seconds while I processed what my cat had just offered up. "Yes. That is correct. Thank you."

"Noooo problem."

"Ooookay, on that note I'm going to the basement to fix up some hairy freaks and then kick their asses out. You want to come?" I asked Fabio.

"Nooooooo, I'll let youuuu handle it on youur oooown."

Chapter 6

I expected the bear to have pooped a mountain and all hell to have broken loose in the basement. I was wrong—so very wrong. For a brief moment I considered screaming, then I contemplated transporting the hell out of West Virginia. Finally I weighed how stupid it would be to blow up the house and call it a day. In the end curiosity won out.

"Um, where is my zoo and who in the hell are you naked people?" The cages were now filled with two stark naked women, three nude men and a beautiful little boy who couldn't have been more than four. And they all started talking at once.

I was able to make out the words *Hildy, new one, Shifter wars* and *I have to go to the can.* They were Shifters? What in the hell did Shifters want with me?

"Shut up!" I shouted. They went silent and waited. "One at a time you will tell me your name and what happened to you—then I will hold a short press conference to either answer your questions truthfully or lie if I don't know the answer. I will then attempt to do a little magic juju on you to fix up your booboos, and you will all go home to your pack or tribe or gaggle. Clear?"

"My name is Chuck," the now human bear said in a deep gravelly voice. "I really have to take a crap and would greatly appreciate the use of your facilities. Now."

"What happened to you?" I asked as I ransacked the bins of clothes and threw him the largest pair of pants I could find. The dude was freakin' huge and seriously good looking. He had to be at least seven feet tall.

"Turf war with the panthers. Bathroom?" he grunted.

"Upstairs on the left. If you clog the toilet I'll smite your ass."

"Got it," he said as he took the stairs three at a time.

"You." I pointed at what used to be the beaver as I tossed him some clothes. He was short and muscular and had a hairline that started right above his nose. That was unfortunate and I wondered if he'd ever thought about electrolysis. "Story."

"My name is Bob," he said in a soft voice. That would be easy to remember... Bob the beaver. "My shoal was attacked by coyotes and my alpha was killed. We are scattered in caves and gullies along the river. I need healing and then I need to get back to my people. Please."

"Um... sure," I said. Bob beamed and dropped to his knees in gratitude. "Let me just get everyone's names and then I'll, you know, give you a tune up. Cool?"

He nodded and got to his feet.

"My name is Deedee," the very naked and very pretty deer shifter told me. Her huge hazel eyes filled with tears as she went on. "My herd has been dwindling for a while and my mate was killed by mortal hunters for sport. We hid and buried his body, but we are relocating. I am wounded and unable to make the trip. That is why I am here, your grace."

"It's Zelda," I corrected her.

"She was bestowing you with a complimentary title to butter you up," a wiry little dude sporting a shock of black hair with a white stripe down the middle informed me.

"Yes, well, I am not grace or graceful or even all that nice, so Zelda will do," I snapped, a little embarrassed that the honor flew right over my head. "You're the skunk."

"Yes." He grinned and I had to bite back a giggle. He was cute and bizarre and if he didn't blow stinkbombs out of his butt, we could have been friends. "My name is

Simon and I'm not actually injured at all. I was just ensuring a safe passage for Wanda and BoboBabyBoy."

"Mmmmkay."

I glanced over at what I assumed was the mother raccoon and her baby. Damn it to hell he *was* cute, but what a name.

"I'm sorry, what's his name?" I asked, sure I'd misunderstood.

"It's BoboBabyBoy," Wanda said as she stroked the small, beautiful child's hair.

"Is that all one word?"

"Yes, of course." She smiled and nodded.

"Wow, you do realize he's going to get his ass kicked in school with a name like that."

"BoboBabyBoy is an alpha," she explained, as if that negated the most redonkulous name I'd ever heard.

"That's great and all, but he's still going to get his butt handed to him at least three times a week and six times on the weekends," I told her.

Wanda's eyes grew wide and she pulled BoboBabyBoy close. She was seconds away from bursting into tears. Fuck, I needed to learn tact, but feared it was far too late for me to develop any social skills.

"What's his real name?" I asked, praying to the Goddess it wasn't BoboBabyBoy.

"Beauregard."

Damn... not much better. "Why don't you call him Bo? It's strong and no one will want a piece of a raccoon alpha named Bo." At least I didn't think they would.

Wanda glanced around at the other Shifters who nodded in agreement. "Do you think that would work?" she asked me, still clutching the boy to her.

"I do."

"Then we shall call him Bo." She leaned down and kissed and hugged the little boy lovingly. I felt a burning pang of jealously settle in my gut. My mother had barely touched me. Ever.

Turning away from something I couldn't relate to, I got back to the matter at hand.

"Do you have a plunger?" Chuck the bear called from the top of the stairs.

"Are you serious?" I shouted. He was now my enemy. It didn't matter how handsome he was.

"Nahhhhh." He laughed as he loped back to the group. "Just screwing with ya."

I rolled my eyes and took in the motley crew. They were injured and they looked weak and tired. "I'm guessing my Aunt Hildy used to fix you hairy bastards up?"

"She was the Shifter Whisperer," Deedee said reverently. "And now you are."

"Nope, I'm just here for a month, so I don't get put back in the pokey or turned into a mortal. I am not the Shifter Whipper."

"Whisperer," Little Bo said in an adorable voice.

I wanted to squeeze him. Hard.

"Whipper, whisperer, whatever... it's not me. I'm a materialistic witch who isn't even crazy about animals. Sooooo I am *not* your gal."

"This is the new Shifter Whisperer?" Bob demanded in a disgusted voice. "Worthless," he muttered under his breath.

"Bob, while I kind of understand your disappointment, if you're an assbucket I won't heal you and I might even lower your hair line by an inch or two."

I smiled and hopped up on the metal table. Bob the beaver gasped and moved behind Chuck the bear.

"Now line up and get ready to be zapped."

Quickly they all began to strip out of the clothes I'd just given them. WTF? As soon as they were in the buff they all shifted back to their animal form except for Simon the buttbomb maker.

"Is there a reason we need to be in zoo form for healing?" I asked the one uninjured member of the fur pack.

"Oh yes, you'll be able to communicate much better with them in their shifted forms," Simon explained and hopped up on the table next to me.

"And more importantly, is there a reason you're buck ass naked?"

I stared at the ceiling and prayed I didn't accidentally on purpose smite all the annoying species in my basement.

"Whoops." He giggled and re-dressed himself.

"Who's first?" I asked as I rolled my neck and popped my knuckles. I could do this. Healing had always come easily to me. I tended not to let people know because I didn't want to have to deal with it. My mom couldn't heal a flea and I spent most of my childhood fixing her every ache and pain. Did this make her love me? No. Would I do it over? Probably. Pathetic and in need of a mommy didn't make for well-adjusted adults.

Deedee the deer stepped forward and stared at me intently. Her head swung gracefully from left to right and her eyes never left mine for a moment.

"What the hell is she doing?" I asked Simon.

"Talking to you. Listen."

"I already told you dumbasses I am not the Shifter Whisperer. I am Zelda the slightly unstable and selfish witch. You're going to have to interpret for her or we're all up shit's creek."

"Listen," Simon insisted. "Open your pea brain and listen."

"You're a dick," I told him. "I said I was selfish, not stupid."

"My bad. Listen. Please."

I rolled my eyes and closed them. These Shifters were nuts. They were asking me to be someone I wasn't.

I listened.

Nothing.

I listened harder.

Nothing.

"I can't do this," I said. "I don't hear anything. I'm sorry."

The group looked at me in confusion. I shrugged and got up to leave. I was sick and tired of being a disappointment to everyone. Maybe being a mortal *was* the answer.

"You're her niece," Simon said. "You have her blood."

"Who? Hildy?" I stopped and turned back. "I don't know if I'm really her niece. I didn't even know she existed till the other day. There is no proof. None. I'm sorry to tell you this, but you have the wrong gal."

"No," Simon yelled, startling me. "You look just like her and we feel your magic. You. Are. The. Shifter. Whisperer."

"No," I shot back. "I. Am. Zelda. The. Fuck. Up."

I was done. I didn't even care if Baba Yaga sent me back to the pokey. I didn't glance back as I made my way to the stairs. I couldn't. I'd find Fabio a witch that would be good to him and overlook his crotch goblin habit. I'd drive the ugly green piece of crap right back to Salem, check myself back into jail and wait for Halloween and my mortal status. I would mope and watch TV. Good plan.

"*You really are the Shifter Whisperer. You have to believe... we do,*" a female voice implored.

I jerked to a stop and whipped around. "Who said that?" I demanded, looking around for a woman not in furry form.

"*I did,*" DeeDee the damn deer said. "*And you heard me.*"

I did. I didn't want to, but I did. They all knew it evidenced by the hopping around and peeing on the walls.

"Absolutely not," I yelled at Chuck, who had peed on the wall and looked suspiciously like he was going to add a dump to that. "Yes, I heard you, but if you defecate in my house I will ignore all of you. Permanently."

The ruckus stopped and the animals shivered in anticipation. Fuckityfuckfuck, now what was I supposed to do?

"*My injuries are in my front left leg,*" DeeDee told me. It was odd. Her mouth didn't move like Fabio's did when he spoke. It was like a weird mindmeld thing. Very *Star Trek*. "*I think it's fractured.*"

"I thought Shifters could heal themselves," I said to Simon as I ran my hand through my hair nervously.

"She has already healed herself substantially. She has nothing left and that's where you come in," he said as he bowed to me.

"Don't do that," I snapped. "It makes me uncomfortable." What if I couldn't do it?

"As you wish." He grinned and winked. I was beginning to really like the skunk.

I squatted down and examined DeeDee's leg. Sure enough, it jutted out the wrong way. Small pieces of sharp bone covered in dried blood protruded through her light brown fur. Magic took me without my calling it up. It was alarming, but I went with it. It was warm and swirled around me stronger than it ever had. Lavender sparks crackled and bounced around. My hair flew around my head and I laughed—with joy. Nothing had ever felt so right.

I gently touched her leg and I went from elated to shocked so quickly I fell backward. Her leg healed, but there was a price. A burning shot of pain exploded through my own leg that mimicked the area of her injury. Shit. The heat eased, but I was a little wary to find out where everyone else was injured...especially Chuck.

"Well, that sucked," I said as I massaged my leg. "Chuck, if you're having bowel problems you are shit out of luck for a healing. Pun intended."

"*My wound is on my shoulder. There is a bullet lodged deep,*" he said as he showed me the hole. "*If you would remove the bullet I will be on my way.*"

"Can I just reach in and pull it out?" I asked Simon. I knew I might puke, but it would save my shoulder a world of pain if I could fix Chuck without magic.

"Nope," Simon informed me, way too happily for my pleasure.

He was a sick bastard.

"Fine," I ground out. "Chuck, sit. You're too damned tall for me to reach you standing. And I mean sit—not squat."

I heard Chuck's laughter rumble around in my head as he plopped down on the floor. Again, the magic came up unbidden as soon as I touched him... and again it hurt like a motherfucker. Maybe Hildy hadn't died. Maybe she got sick of being in excruciating pain all the time and just took off. They never did find a body.

"Next," I gasped as the bullet popped out of Chuck's shoulder. Better to get it all over fast before I chickened out.

Bob had a partially cut artery and Wanda had broken paws and her femur was cracked. It was getting difficult to breathe or even see straight, but Baby Bo was still waiting.

"I can do one more," I told them. "Come here, little guy."

He scampered over and curled up in my lap. My heart grew three sizes like the freakin' Grinch as I nuzzled his slightly stinky fur.

"*My head hurts,*" he said. "*It hurts so bad, Zelda.*"

Blood still slowly seeped from a long gash at the base of his little skull and my inside clenched in fury. He was just a little boy.

"What happened to him?" I demanded.

"He was attacked by honey badgers and thrown against a tree," Simon said quietly. A very pale and now healed Wanda shifted back to human and sat next to me on the floor. All of the animals had shifted back and were dressing themselves as they watched.

"What the hell is wrong with you Shifters? Why would anyone attack a child?"

"Territory," Chuck grunted in disgust. "When Hildy was killed her magic left the area and all the species are vying for territory."

"Is this entire town Shifters?" I asked as I absently rubbed little Bo's soft tummy.

"Yes," DeeDee offered. "Mortals may stop in town, but they never stay. We have made it as unappealing as possible."

"Your grocery store sucks," I said as an image of Hot Ass Guy popped back into my brain. I wondered if he was a Shifter or a mortal passing through.

"Go to the back of the store and through the supply door. That's where all the good food is kept." Bob let me in on the secret. "There is a whole store within the store."

"Tell Fabio that. He's the one with the bad credit cards and the need to shop for food."

"Will do," Bob said.

"All right, I don't suppose I'll know what's going on inside of Bo until I touch his wound. Back up guys, I have a feeling this one is bad."

I was right.

But I had no idea how right I was.

Baby Bo had a brain injury with internal bleeding. The rocket blast of searing pain that crunched my brain was indescribable. I gasped for air as I tried to let my magic flow from my body to his. His large brown eyes held mine as tears seeped from them.

If I ever came across a honey badger I would smite it dead so fast it wouldn't know what hit him. Bursts of color exploded in my head and I knew I shook like a leaf. I could hold on for a little bit longer. All I needed was to feel the click… hang on—just hang on.

The click came slowly. I'd healed the baby.

I tried to smile afterward, but it formed on my face like a pained grimace. My entire body ached. I vaguely heard cheering in the distance, but my body was behaving like it was in quicksand. I attempted to stand, but the room was spinning and I floated above myself. I tried to explain that this job wasn't going to work out for me. However, it sounded like mushy Martian, even to my own ears. The wide-eyed and worried looks on the faces of my patients concerned me a bit, but at least I was done.

And then everything went black.

Chapter 7

My mouth tasted like rank sandpaper and I'd never had to pee so badly in my life. However, the main problem was prying my eyes open. They were stuck.

"Is sheeeeeee awake?" Fabio asked frantically.

"She's waking up," Simon burst out with relieved excitement. "Wanda, go and get some water and some broth. Quickly."

"Pizza," I mumbled. "I want pizza and a half Coke, half diet Coke. I'm living on the edge."

"I'm on it," Wanda said.

I heard footsteps race from the room, but my damn eyes were still cemented shut.

"Zeeeeelda, I think I lost four liiiives in the past twooooo weeks worrying about youuuuuuuuuuuu."

Two weeks? I'd been out for two weeks? No wonder my mouth tasted like butt.

"Pee. I have to pee. Now." I pried my eyes open with my fingers and immediately shut them again because the light in the room gave me a mini migraine. "Help me to the bathroom and do not get in the vicinity of my mouth. You will die."

"I've got her," Simon said as he carefully led me across the room and into the bathroom.

"Out," I instructed as I began peeling my clothes from my body. "I am going to pee for twenty-seven minutes, and then I'm going to shower for forty-two minutes, followed by scrubbing my teeth for sixty-one minutes. After that I will come out. If you could get me some clean clothes, you can have my first child if I ever get over my fear of commitment. Deal?"

"Deal." Simon laughed as he shut the door behind him.

I was shaky, but the pee, shower and brush were so satisfying, I made it work. Had I really been out for two weeks? Shit. It was getting closer to Halloween and I still had no real clue what I was doing here.

I made my way back to my bedroom dressed in a fabu Max Midnight mini, a tight chocolate camisole and a killer pair of Prada flats that Fabio must have stolen while I was out of commission. At least I looked good. Plus I would no longer asphyxiate someone with my breath.

"So," I said as I greeted my audience that consisted of Fabio, Simon, Wanda and a happy and healthy little Bo. "I've been out for two weeks?"

"Yes," Bo said as he threw his tiny body at mine and hugged my leg as if his life depended on it.

"I do believe," I said as I stared pointedly at Simon, "that this proves I am not the Shifter Whopper."

"Whisperer," Bo corrected me sweetly.

"Right. Anyhoo, I think you guys might want to put an ad on Craigslist or get the word out that you need a healer who is into sadomasochism because that shit hurt."

Concerned glances passed between all the occupants in the room except for me.

"Iiiiit won't always be that baaaaad," Fabio purred as he rubbed himself on my legs that I'd just expertly shaved.

"And you know this how?" I narrowed my eyes at him and waited.

The little bastard huffed out a put-upon sigh and glanced longingly at his balls.

"If you even peek at your nuts again before you answer me I will magically remove them," I warned.

I seated myself and grabbed a hot slice of pizza Wanda had made. Goddess, it tasted good.

"I knoooooow this because I kneeew that woman Hildy when she started. Each time sheeeeee healed others, it took less tolllllll and she became more powerful."

The more powerful thing was appealing because I was alarmingly shallow, but I wasn't sure I believed the pain would ever lessen.

"I'm not entirely buying that shit, Fabio. And there is far more to that story," I told him as wolfed down a second slice. "All I know is my magic ass is grass if I don't find my mission and solve it."

"Have you considered *this* may be your mission?" Simon inquired casually.

"Nope. I was not meant to live with Shifters in Assjacket, West Virginia for the rest of my life. I mean, you people don't even have a mall, much less a Target. I'm not into pain and I don't have a TV."

"Yes, you do! A humongous one," Bo said. "I've been watching cartoons for two weeks straight."

One issue solved. "Whatever. I'm not the one you need."

"But you're the one we want," Wanda said quietly. "Hildy was wonderful, but you... you're a little crazy. In a good way," she added quickly.

An unlady-like snort escaped my lips. "You want a crazy witch who doesn't like animals to be your Shifter Whoosher?"

"Yes, Zelda, we do," Bo said with a huge smile on his face. He was missing his two front teeth. I had to look away it was so damn cute.

"Where are Chuck, Bob and DeeDee?" I asked as I sipped my icy cold soda.

"They left after you healed them, but they've checked in daily. Actually Chuck is downstairs," Simon answered as he handed me a third slice. He was a sly one.

"Thank you," I said with a mouthful. "Do any of you know how Hildy was killed?"

I decided getting right to the point would save time considering I didn't have a whole bunch left.

"We're unsure, but we know it was violent," Wanda said as she held out a fourth piece.

"No, thanks. I'm good," I told her. They were a smart bunch. Bribing me with pizza was crafty. "I've heard about the violent part. How do you guys know it was violent if there was no body?"

Again, nervous glances were exchanged.

"Look, if someone killed the former Shifter Wanker, don't you think it would be nice if I have some idea of who or what might come after me?"

"So you accept your fate? You believe you are the Wanker?" Simon asked.

"Did you just call me a wanker?"

"You said it first." His grin almost split his face.

"Point," I agreed as I grinned back. "And no. I accept nothing. I'm just not in the mood to be offed anytime soon. So spill."

"There was blood—lots of blood all over Hildy's kitchen," Bo said.

"And her magic left the area after we found the blood," Wanda added sadly.

That didn't sound good. I hopped up and began to pace the room in agitation. I didn't have time for vague crap. I had a stupid ass mission to accomplish or I was going to become a mortal.

Unacceptable.

"Did she have enemies?"

"No more than anyone else," Simon said as Fabio rolled his eyes.

I halted abruptly and turned on Fabio. "Cat, start talking."

"Fiiiine. Hiiiildy was a menace. She liked to stir up trouble since the daaay she was hatched," he hissed.

"I thought she was a witch."

"Oh, she was, but she was a little on the unstable side," Simon added. "In a good way."

"Let me get this straight. She was basically an insanely imbalanced witch who courted trouble, fixed furballs and kept some kind of magical balance in the area?"

"She also was quite the fashion plate," Simon chimed in.

"Don't you see how perfect you are for the job?" Wanda shouted enthusiastically.

"Um, Wanda, you're not really helping here," I told her.

Yes, I was insane. Yes, some would describe me as an unbalanced trouble magnet. Yes, I could heal and yes, I was well dressed... but shit. I didn't want to do this.

"Theeeere are more in the baaasement," Fabio said as he delicately picked at the piece of pizza I'd declined.

"More what?"

"Moooooore injured Shifters, but you are too weak to fix theeeeeem."

"Son of a bitch. How wounded are they?" I demanded as I rushed to the door. "And how many?"

Simon grinned and elbowed an also grinning Wanda.

"Cut that shit out," I snapped. "I don't want dead animals in the basement. It'll stink. I am not the Wanker, but I will see if I can help the bastards in the dungeon. Capisce?"

"Whatever you say," Simon said. "Follow me."

There were four and they were in bad shape. Chuck the bear was among them. He was knocked out and bleeding badly. Clearly he was a fucking idiot. Shit. My stomach lurched at the thought I might be passed out for another two weeks, but the Shifters would most certainly die if I didn't help them.

"You assbuckets need to stop trying to kill each other," I admonished the new group. "I have about had it."

"*Will she help us?*" a mountain lion asked Simon. "*Is she capable?*"

"*She looks kind of off,*" a bloody wolf added.

"*Actually, I'd say she's crazy,*" a mangled rabbit chimed in.

Of course Chuck was silent as he was out like a light.

"I can hear you," I shouted, scaring the crap out of everyone, including Fabio, who jumped so high I laughed. "If you're going to talk about me I'd suggest you speak Russian or French. I don't speak those languages and your insults will fly right over my head. If I don't realize you're mocking me I might not spay or neuter you in the process of your healing. However, since you're stupid enough to have been discourteous, all bets are off as far as your reproductive organs go."

"*Is she serious?*" the wolf asked, aghast.

"*I think she's hot,*" the mountain lion grunted.

"*Yes, hot, but definitely serious,*" the rabbit tittered in a horrified voice.

"Thank you, O Great Lion. You shall keep your scrotum. The rest of you—it's a maybe at best. Now get your bloody carcasses over here and let me have at you."

The menagerie slowly lined up and dragged the incapacitated Chuck with them. They waited in a terrified line for me to do my voodoo. I kind of liked the power I had over them until I had to actually heal them.

Thankfully Fabio was correct. It was easier this time, but it still hurt like a bitch. After repairing the lion's throat, the wolf's heart, the rabbit's entire body and Chuck's gaping head wound, I was nauseous and dizzy. But I was also awake and in full possession of my body.

"All right, get out of here unless you need to sleep or something," I told them. I didn't want the new guys' names. I was getting too attached to the Shifters from the first round of healing. I was going to make a clean break here soon and having feelings for people who turned into animals was not going to help.

"Youuuuu did goood, Zeeelda," Fabio said as he pushed me with his little paw toward a pile of bags in the corner of the basement.

"What are those?" I asked as I eyed the large shopping bags labeled Prada and Gucci and Barney's.

"We came bearing gifts for the Shifter Whisperer," the lion, now a very handsome man, said.

Thankfully he'd donned some pants and a shirt or I might have started drooling. Between him and the now conscious Chuck the bear the basement was beginning to look like a hot dude strip club.

"We heard you enjoy designer duds," the lion explained.

"That's very kind of you," I said. It was difficult, but I held myself back from diving on the bags and tearing them open. "Is this how you, um... paid my Aunt Hildy?"

I could possibly live with this.

Chuck, now in full possession of his voice, shifted back and forth uncomfortably. "Um, no. I usually just bent her over the chair and..."

"Enough!" Simon cut him off before he illuminated the room with details about my dead aunt's sex life.

Nice. I was definitely no longer attracted to the bear who had clearly popped my aunt.

"Sheeeeee was a sluuuuut like your motheeer," Fabio announced.

"I do believe I already told you that I'm the only one who is allowed to bust on my mother's morals." I heaved out a sigh and paced the room. What I really needed was to get the hell out of the house and breathe some fresh air. "I'm going for a walk."

"We'll come with you," Wanda offered quickly.

"Actually, Wanda, I want to be alone."

"Is that safe?" she whispered to Simon.

"What are you talking about?" I demanded.

"It's fine," Simon assured me and the other Shifters nodded. "Your land is being patrolled by Mac and several other wolves."

All of the Shifters bowed their heads in deference to this Mac dude.

Well, all right then. I was getting the hell out for a bit. Mac and his posse clearly had it under control.

Chapter 8

I was definitely *not* getting attached to the place, but I had to admit Assbuckle, West Virginia was beautiful. The leaves were jewel-toned and fall blooms exploded all over the hill as I meandered away from the house. I knew they were all watching me from the windows so I walked farther away than I had planned.

Which of course turned out to be a fantastically stupid idea.

I heard it before I saw it—teeth gnashing, growls and screams. Instead of running away like any normal person would, I ran toward it. I was in no mood to heal any more hairy, bloody bastards. It was time for these idiots to get along.

Holy Hell. It was ugly with a capital U. There had to be at least twenty honey badgers on the one wolf. The wolf was being attacked on every side. He was tearing them apart, but there were entirely too many and they were getting a piece of him with each strike. I watched for a brief moment, then my body jerked into action before my brain could process what a bad plan that might be.

Green and blood red magical fire whooshed up my arms and a fury consumed me. I was certain I looked like a Christmas tree inferno, but this was no time to be vain. Were these the fuckers that had tried to kill little Bo? And now they were after my bodyguard? Hell no. Not on my clock.

I pointed and aimed. Blazing magic flew from my hands to the bad guys. Two honey badgers popped like watermelons when you dropped them off of a five-story building. How did I know this? Easy. I'd been tossing watermelons and other large fruit off buildings since I was a child. Innocent fun had been difficult to come by as a young witch...

The wolf glanced over in shock for a moment and then went back to his fight with a viciousness that left me a bit breathless. I sure as hell hoped he was the good guy because I was popping badgers like I popped bubble wrap. Between the two of us I was fairly sure we were winning.

It was all going swimmingly until my aim went awry and I zapped the wolf in the ass.

"Shit," I screamed as I watched him drop to the ground with a thud. At least he didn't pop.

The honey badgers that remained dove on him while several ran at full speed toward me. As soon as I was done here I was leaving this town. For real.

I lifted my arms and chanted to the Goddess.

"Evil is as evil does.
Help me save the day.
Take from this Earth the ones who sin.
Make them go away."

In a massive blast of magic each and every honey badger was blown to smithereens and I couldn't have been happier. Violence had never been my forte or desire, but when it came down to me or them I definitely voted for me.

Now for the wolf...

He was huge and smelled like sunshine and wind. WTF? Animals were supposed to stink. Thankfully he was still alive. Even though he was a bloody mess I wanted to bury my face in his fur. However, I needed to get the huge thing out of here. Who knew what else was lurking?

Only one problem... he weighed a ton.

I considered going back for help, but there was no way I was leaving him out here alone and practically dead.

So I dragged him. Magic helped, but I was a bit depleted from my honey badger kill-fest. I was sweating and got his blood on my mini skirt. That was unacceptable. I needed to zap myself into a clean skirt, but that would be using my magic incorrectly according to Bumpy Yumpy. I hated Bumpy Yumpy.

Thirty minutes later and now sporting blood on my Prada flats and chocolate cami, I was pissed. But I was home.

"Get your asses out here and help me," I shouted.

Simon, Wanda, Bo, Fabio, Chuck and the trio I didn't want to know the names of came flying out of the house.

"Ohhhhhhh myyyyyy Goddesssss, what happened?" Fabio screeched.

"Honey badgers happened," I hissed.

"And you're still alive?" the rabbit asked.

"Apparently. And I sure as hell hope there are some flats in that Prada bag you brought because I ruined these. Help me get this damn wolf to the basement."

Fabio came right to my side, but the others were frozen in shock. As Fab would be of little help dragging the wolf, I slapped my hands on my hips and stared down the crowd.

"Did you stop speaking English while I was out popping honey badgers?" I demanded.

"You popped them?" the mountain lion asked, impressed.

"Like ticks. Now help me."

"That's Mac," the rabbit gasped. "What happened to him?"

"I had bad aim and I zapped him by accident," I explained to the flabbergasted group. "What? I didn't mean to."

"He's gonna be mad." The wolf I'd healed was grinning from ear to ear.

"And that's funny?" I ground out.

"Yep," he answered. "Very funny."

"Whatever. Just help me bring him to the basement."

"I think it would be better and more appropriate if we took him to a bedroom," Simon volunteered. He had gone pale and was shaking.

"Absolutely not. He may smell really good, but he's bleeding like a stuck pig and I am not doing laundry. He goes to the basement or he can bite it on the front lawn."

"You think he smells good?" Chuck asked, surprised.

All the damn Shifters tried to bite back delighted smiles. What was going on here?

"Yes. He smells good. So what?"

"Describe it," the mountain lion insisted gleefully.

"Oh my Goddess, this is so dumb. He smells like sunshine and wind. You want to know anything else while he bleeds out on the grass?"

"Nope." The mountain lion, wolf and Chuck the bear were positively ecstatic. They picked the wounded wolf up, took him to the basement and locked him in a cage.

"Is that really necessary?" I asked. "You can just leave him on the floor. You don't have to lock him up like a convict."

"Zeeelda just spent nine months in the pokey for killing meeeee," Fabio explained to a now confused crowd.

"TMI, dude," I told my cat. "Seriously, don't lock him up."

I had no clue why locking the wolf up bothered me but it did.

"Trust me," the rabbit chimed in. "It will be better for everyone if he's incarcerated when he wakes up."

The Shifters all moved quickly to the stairs and right out the front door, including Simon, Chuck, Wanda and Bo.

"Um, is there a reason you all are leaving so soon?" I asked, now somewhat uncomfortable and more than a little freaked out. "Is he going to want kill me or something like that?"

"Hell no," my mountain lion buddy said. "He won't harm a hair on your head. We just think you'll need some privacy."

With that cryptic message they fled. It was me and Fabio against the world...and the wolf.

61

"Was that as weird as I think it was?" I asked him.

"I'd haaave to say yesssss."

"Okay, good, because I'd hate to think I was crazy."

"Ohhhh, you're crazy, buuut that was odd."

"You're a pain in my ass," I told him as I flopped down on the couch and went for the remote of the lovely ginormous flat screen TV.

"Thaank youuuu. Can weeee watch Animal Planet?"

"No. No, we can't. Nice try though."

"How abooout *Say Yes to the Dresssssssss*?"

"Now you're talking."

Chapter 9

I jerked up and gasped as I wiped the drool from my mouth. I had clearly fallen asleep. Dragging several hundred pounds of wolf and getting bled on can do that to a girl. Fabio was on my head and the racket coming from the basement made me shudder. The wolf was awake and he wasn't happy.

His bellowing was ear splitting and it was giving me a headache. Obviously he had shifted back to human form and was pissed. Suddenly it seemed like a very good idea that he was locked up, but if the violent cage rattling was any indication he wouldn't be locked up for long.

Shitshitshit.

"What do I do?" I hissed at Fabio as I pulled him off my head.

"Ruuun?" he suggested.

His recommendation had merit and I considered it for eight seconds, but when the shouting got even louder I got mad.

"I saved that stupid wolf's life. He is not going to give me a migraine," I groused as I got to my feet. "You coming?"

"Oooonly if youuuuu make me," he said.

"You're worthless," I muttered as I stomped to the door of the basement. I'd had enough of this crap. At least the last group I'd saved had brought me presents. This jackass was just loud and ungrateful.

ROBYN PETERMAN

"Let me out of here. Now," a deep and strangely familiar voice bellowed.

"If you would shut your cakehole for two seconds I might," I yelled as I rounded the corner and marched angrily into the room only to stop short and gape.

It was Hot Ass Guy from the grocery store and he was naked. About six feet four of total, furious buck ass naked perfection enthralled me and I couldn't move. His eyes narrowed dangerously as he took me in.

"I should have known it was you," he muttered disgustedly.

"Listen, you unappreciative asswaffle, you need to change that crappy attitude or I'll leave you in that cage," I shot back. I also tried like hell not to stare at his truly spectacular package.

"Did you just call me an asswaffle?" he asked in shock.

"Yes, I did...because you are."

"My eyes are up here," he countered dryly.

I felt the heat crawl up my neck and land on my cheeks as I yanked my gaze from his abundant man jewels to his face.

"Can't blame a girl for looking," I informed him, hoping I sounded casual and uninterested. My bored tone was actually pretty good, but my insides were on fire and my lady bits were screaming. Holy Hell, if I let him out there was a fine chance I'd jump him.

"If you release me I'll let you touch it," he offered in a voice that made my knees weak.

"No. You're a pig. I wouldn't touch that thing if you paid me," I snapped. "I'm sure it's had a very active social life."

"First of all I'm a wolf, not a pig—pig shifters don't exist. As far as my Johnson's social life goes, he knows what to do."

He grinned and my panties dampened.

"So you're the new Shifter Whisperer?" he asked doubtfully.

"First of all, you really need to come up with a more original name than Johnson for your weenie, and even if you begged I wouldn't touch that behemoth with a ten foot pole. And no, I am not the new Shifter Woowoohoodoo. I'm just filling in until you idiots find a permanent replacement. Now if you want me to fix you, you will have to cover your *Johnson* or shift back to wolf."

"Come here," he said softly.

"Um... I don't think that's a good plan," I mumbled as I fought to unlock my green eyes from staring into his sapphire blue ones.

"Come here," he repeated softly.

Son of a bitch, his voice was like honey and he smelled like heaven. My body yet again took over for my brain. I walked toward the wolf like a moth to a flame.

As I approached his eyes grew wide and he sniffed the air. He winced and pinched the bridge of his nose.

"Stop that. I do not smell bad," I snapped just before I angrily walked to the cage and poked him. "You are rude and I might not fix you."

He grabbed my hand and pinned me against the cage. "This is not happening," he muttered. "This cannot be happening."

"You may be hot but you're weird...and you're scaring me. Let me go. *Now*."

I tried to jerk away but he held me fast. His scent was making me dizzy and my stomach was hosting a track meet. I needed to get away from him. Quickly.

"Open the cage, Zelda."

He was very sexy and I was very horny. Not a good combo.

"Nope, and how do you know my name?"

"Your Aunt Hildy spoke of you often," he said. His grip lessened but still kept me trapped.

"Oh my Goddess," I grumbled, hating my aunt. "Did you do her too?"

"Don't talk about her like that," he ground out through clenched teeth. "She was like a mother to me."

"Awesome," I yelled, completely relieved that he hadn't humped Hildy. "Now let me go or I won't heal you."

"I wouldn't need you to heal me if you hadn't zapped my ass with a volt that should have killed me." He raised

65

his eyebrows, obviously waiting for an apology. It was never coming in this lifetime.

"I saved your hairy butt, you unthankful jerk," I informed him as my eyebrows shot higher than his.

"I was doing fine until you showed up."

His arrogance made me grind my teeth.

"Right." I rolled my eyes. "It certainly looked that way with twenty honey badgers taking a bite out of you."

"I was minutes away from destroying them when you jumped in. You could have died," he accused.

"Yes, but instead I popped all the fuckers and dragged your sorry ass here. You bled on my Prada and Max Midnight. I don't like you."

"Who is Max Midnight?" he demanded as he pulled me closer. His eyes were wild and it was sexier than hell. I had to hold my tongue so I didn't beg to touch his damn Johnson.

"My miniskirt, you asshole."

"It's not your lover?" he asked as he calmed a little.

WTF? Was he jealous?

"Um… no."

"Do you have a lover?"

"I really don't see how that's any of your business, Wolf Boy. Do you have one?"

The question flew from my lips before I could stop it. Alarmingly, I realized if he said yes I would get her name and go kill her.

Wait. What was going on here?

"As of a moment ago I'm off the market," he said as he watched me closely.

"That makes no sense, Little Mister. However, if you don't let go of me I will smite your sorry ass and you won't fucking live through it this time."

"Nice mouth." His grin was intoxicating. I wanted to bite on his full lips and ride him like a cowboy. There was no way in Hell I was letting him out.

"Thank you—I try. Now let go."

"Unlock the cage and I'll let you go," he bargained.

It was either a lose-lose scenario or a win-win depending on how you looked at it. I was not a virgin, but

66

I'd never been so wildly attracted to anyone in my life. I was sure there was some kind of Witch-o-cratic oath that stated I couldn't have hot monkey sex with my patients.

Decisions sucked.

"No. I think that's a bad idea," I said as my traitorous body leaned closer to the cage and the beautiful, dangerous man inside.

"It's an incredibly bad idea," he agreed. "But you will do it."

"Will you hurt me?" I whispered, mesmerized by his mouth.

"Only if you're into that," he replied just as quietly. "Personally I'm not into pain, but if it makes you happy…"

"Um, no. I'm not really into that. A spanking is nice, but…" I slapped my hand over my mouth and groaned in mortification.

His sexy chuckle made me clench my thighs together.

"What are you doing to me?" I asked as I futilely tried to wiggle out of his iron grip. Did werewolves have magic I wasn't aware of? I'd always had a healthy sex life with absolutely no commitment, but this was nuts. I was naming our children in my head. He had to have cast a spell on me.

"The same thing you're doing to me," he told me. "I'm not sure I like it, but I have very little control over it."

"I think I was just insulted," I huffed in exasperation when I finally was able to yank myself free. "You've spelled me or something."

"Or something," he agreed and ran his free hand through his thick dark hair.

"Look, just shift back to wolf, I'll fix you and you can leave. Forever."

He paced the cage and my eyes were glued to the rippling muscles in his thighs and ass. No one had the right to look like him. He was gorgeous. I was in trouble.

"You're my mate," Mac said as he shook his head in confusion.

WTF?

"And you're on crack. I'm a witch and you're a wolf. I was not built to blow puppies out of my hooha."

His eyes shot to mine and a burst of laughter came out of him. "You did not just say that."

"I most certainly did, so turn off the testosterone and get that redonkulous idea out of your head. Immediately."

"As much as I'm at loath to admit it, I do need your help. I'll shift and then you can let me out of the cage. Deal?"

He did look beat up...and I did zap his ass. If he was in wolf form I wouldn't tackle him. This could work. Maybe...

"Shift first," I told him. "And then I'll let you out."

He shrugged and shifted. It was beautiful to watch. His wolf was large. His fur was the same chocolate brown as his hair and his eyes were the exact same mesmerizing blue. I was still mystified as to why he smelled so delicious, but ignored all the warning bells in my head.

I focused on the goal. Fix the hot guy and get rid of him. Wolf Boy was nothing but trouble.

I approached him slowly just in case he was screwing with me and shifted back. I knew I couldn't be trusted if he was in his human form. He was just too pretty.

My spleen is damaged. Touch my back. That should work and if you're feeling generous, my ass is extremely sore from your magic...

His wolf winked at me and I giggled.

"Tough shit about your ass." I grinned as I laid my hands on his back and then quickly contracted in horrific pain. I sucked in a huge breath and let the lavender magic consume my body and flow into his. My breathing grew labored and I felt lightheaded. He was badly injured and needed me. He twisted in agony beneath my touch, but I hung onto him for dear life. It hurt like hell. I really wasn't cut out for this selfless crap.

I heard and felt a click as his insides mended. I dropped to the floor next to him, put my hands over my eyes and fought to catch my breath.

"Are you all right, Zelda?" His voice was troubled and he nudged me with his cold wet nose.

"Sure. Fucking awesome," I grunted as the dizziness abated. "I did my part. Now you leave."

"*Go to the other side of the room,*" he instructed. "*I'm going to shift and I don't trust myself with you.*"

Hell, *he* didn't trust himself? We were in trouble here. I scampered across the room and waited.

The shift was quick and he looked much healthier and bigger than he had in the cage. My instinct was to throw myself into his strong arms, but I held back.

"You do realize you're mine," he said as he watched me warily.

"I belong to no one but myself. I don't even like you."

"I'm not sure I like you much either," he replied. "But I have never wanted anyone so badly in my life."

"Ditto," I said as I slowly eased my camisole over my head.

"What are you doing?" His voice was pained as he watched. I could feel with every fiber of my being he was seconds away from snapping and attacking me.

"Honestly, I have no idea. My brain says to run, but my lady parts and the rest of my body are insisting on a different plan of action."

His eyes hooded and he watched me with rapt attention. "If you remove any more of your clothing I will take that as an invitation."

"To what?" I purred as I kicked out of my shoes and wondered what the hell had gotten into me.

"To fuck you senseless."

My knees buckled for real at his blunt statement and I held onto the wall for purchase. As badly as I wanted to tear off my skirt and wear it on my head I stopped. "You eat with that mouth?"

"Why don't you come over here and find out?" he suggested. He leaned back on the wall and crossed his massive arms over his muscular chest.

"Okay, how about a deal?" I needed to control this situation or I was going to drown.

"Lay it out," he said with a smirk that I wanted to smack off his face.

"We are clearly attracted to each other, so I propose we get each other out of our systems."

"And how exactly do we do that?"

"We have no strings attached sex and then we call it a day."

His smirk turned to a frown and his eyes narrowed to slits. "No strings attached?"

"Um, yes?"

"I don't like those terms," he said smoothly. "No deal."

"Wait. What? You're a freakin' guy. You're the one who should be jumping for joy at my proposition," I yelled. What the hell was wrong with him?

"You're my mate."

"You're an ass. I am no one's mate. If I wasn't about to explode here I'd kick you out and lock the door."

"I have a key."

"Whatever," I shouted. "Do you want to do it or not?"

"Yes, I want to do it," he ground out.

"No strings attached?" I demanded.

"Whatever you say." He shrugged and grinned.

A tiny part of my brain pointed out that he didn't exactly agree with me, but every other part of me told my brain to shut up.

"Fine," I snapped. "Let's get this shit over with."

"Yes. Let's."

Chapter 10

"Come over here," Mac said. His voice was gruff. He was clearly used to being obeyed.

"Nope, you come over here," I shot back.

"I come to no one," he informed me in a tone I didn't like at all.

For a brief second I almost heeded him, but that would have put the power in his court permanently. We were going to start this sucker as equals. Wait. What the hell was I thinking? We weren't starting anything. This was simply a quick roll in the hay—or the basement, as it were. However, I still wasn't going to let him win.

"Well, then, you're going to have a nasty case of blue balls when I go upstairs to my bedroom and have at it with BOB."

He looked like he wanted to kill me. I was very happy I was on the side of the room closest to the stairs.

"Who is Bob?" he shouted. "You said you had no lover."

"I said nothing of the sort and BOB is my battery operated boyfriend, you asshat," I shouted back. Damn, maybe I should have let him think BOB was actually a guy. It might be fun to watch him implode.

"You are treading on thin ice, pretty girl. I don't share."

"You need to get something straight here besides your *Johnson*," I informed him sarcastically. "I am not your mate and I can do what I want."

He stared up at the ceiling and I could have sworn he was praying. Heaving out a huge put-upon sigh, he took one step toward me. "This goes against everything about me, but I will meet you in the middle."

"I can work with that." I grinned triumphantly as I shimmied out of my skirt and panties. His harsh intake of breath was music to my ears. Everything south of my bellybutton clenched in anticipation.

"You're beautiful," he said as we slowly walked to the middle of the room, stalking each other like prey. I had never been so excited or scared at the same time in my life.

"You better tell me you have a raincoat for your Johnson or it's over before we start."

"I'm a werewolf. I can't carry disease and you're a witch so you can't either."

"True," I admitted. I almost salivated over his six pack abs. My hands literally ached to touch him. How did guys like him even exist? "But I am in no mood to get knocked up with a litter. I'm leaving this hellhole in a week."

"We'll see about that, and you're not in heat so unfortunately I can't knock you up at the moment," he explained as he moved closer.

"And how exactly do you know I'm not in heat?" Goddess, he was an animal. I shoved the part about him wanting to knock me up to the area of my brain I called *'don't ever deal with that'*.

"Scent. The same way I know you're my mate."

"That is utter bullshit, Wolf Man Jack."

"It's Mac."

"Fine. Wolf Man Mac, you're crazy. We're having sex because I want to, and if your Johnson's condition is any indication, you do too. We're consenting, non-committed, not-in-a-relationship-adults who are horny. That's all. Period. Do you understand?"

His eyes blazed and I started backing away. Maybe this was a bad idea. He wanted way more than I did. I just wanted a massive orgasm...or three...and possibly a brief snuggle. He wanted puppies. However, my lady bits were singing an aria and my nipples were standing at painful attention.

"Right now I will agree to anything you say." His voice was rough and it sent delighted chills straight to my toes.

"No puppies and no relationship." I'd stopped moving away and stood my ground.

"Whatever you say," he hissed. Then he grabbed me and pulled me flush against his perfect body.

Again, I realized he'd agreed to nothing, but when all my soft melded against all of his hard I ceased to care. I expected him to crush my lips to his and take everything he wanted except my soul, but I couldn't have been more wrong. Slowly his full lips caressed mine as he gently ran his tongue along the seam. When I happily opened to him, his tongue teased mine as his hands expertly discovered my body.

"Oh my Goddess," I moaned as he pinched my nipples between his fingers and nipped at my ear. I returned the favor and tried to memorize every muscle and nuance. The light sprinkling of dark hair on his chest tickled my breasts and I was rubbing against him like a cat in heat. It was virtually impossible to get close enough.

"No foreplay," I begged as I did what I said I would never do. I touched his Johnson, and oh my Goddess what a Johnson it was.

"Do you want to be on top or bottom?" he asked as his strong hands gripped my ass in a hold I knew would leave marks.

"I get a choice?" I giggled until he pressed the heel of his hand against my clit and pushed two fingers inside of me. That's when my brain shorted out.

"I meant for the first round," he said as he knocked a pile of blankets to the floor and pulled me down with him. "I want to go down on you, but if I'm not inside you in the next thirty seconds I think I'll die."

A ball of heat uncoiled in my lower regions and I was fairly sure I was going to come from his voice alone. "Don't die. That would suck."

"Good plan," he said.

He gently laid me beneath him and took my mouth in a kiss that was hotter than any sex I'd had to date. He tasted even better than he smelled and I realized could happily stay lip-locked with him for the rest of my life.

No. Stop. I was lip-locking with no one for the rest of my life...

The sexy sounds coming from deep within his chest made it hard to breathe as I wantonly opened my legs to him.

"I'll try to go slow," he said as he bit down on his bottom lip.

In a haze of almost painful lust I realized I was jealous of his teeth. I wanted to bite his lip. WTF?

"Slow is for weenies," I hissed as he pushed the head of his cock into my very willing and very ready body. However, he was right. He was huge. "Is that thing going to fit?"

His decidedly masculine chuckle shot through me and my body bucked wildly beneath his. "It'll fit," he assured me and he pressed deeper inside. "You were made for me."

"Enough of that talk," I said. "Just do me."

"As the lady wishes." He sheathed himself completely and my body clamped around his like a vise. His lazy and predatory smile sent me over the edge, along with a feeling of fullness that bordered on the line between pleasure and pain.

"Oh my hell," I gasped and he stilled.

"Are you okay, baby?" he whispered in my ear.

"More than okay," I burst out. "Are you just gonna lie there or are you gonna move?"

All bets were now off.

He moved. Oh my Goddess, how he moved. His beautiful mouth pulled into an evil, sexy smirk as his body powered into mine. I was losing all rational thought and I had no clue where he began or where I ended. This was not just sex. It was life changing and I was as terrified as I was turned on.

His breathing was harsh and his eyes blazed as he branded me. I shrieked at the invasion of my body and soul and gave back as good as I was getting.

"If you mate with me I will tear your balls off after I have a mind-shattering orgasm," I panted. The sensitivity was almost too much to bear. My entire body trembled as he took me like the animal he was... and I freakin' loved it.

My need for him was alarming. My nails raked his back and my hips met every thrust with joyful abandon. I wanted to crawl inside him and stay. His face contorted as the speed became something that probably should have killed me dead.

A deafening roar crashed through my head and my own screams of ecstasy sounded distant. However, the mantra being whispered in my ear was clear and as exciting as any words ever uttered.

"Mine. You're mine," Mac repeated in rhythm with his thrusts.

"No," I told him on a ragged breath as my toes curled with passion. "I belong to no one."

His hips pistoned even faster and our lovemaking became frenzied. Our bodies slapped together as our moans and cries tangled. This was the best thing and the worst thing that ever could have happened to me. My magic surrounded us and cocooned us. A rainbow of sparkling mist rained down and made what was already intense absolutely insane.

"Come. *Now*," he demanded.

As much as I wanted to be in control I was no longer there. This man—this wolf—owned me and I would give him whatever he wanted.

I came. *Hard.*

He threw back his head and roared as he joined me, which sent my woowoo into a second violent orgasm. Colorful bursts of sparkles exploded around us. I screamed so loudly I was sure the entire countryside would hear.

"Oh my god," Mac muttered as he tried to catch his breath. "That was unreal."

I was a mute noodle squished underneath a huge wolf-man. "Having a hard time breathing here," I choked out as my body still twitched with mini orgasmic aftershocks.

"Sorry." He chuckled as he rolled over and pulled my naked, weak and very happy body on top of his.

He wrapped his arms around me tightly as I tried to pull away.

"No. Stay with me," he whispered as his eyes bored into mine.

I wasn't sure if he meant right now or forever, but I wasn't going to ask for clarification. It was too scary.

"That was, um… awesome," I blurted out. It was much safer than blurting out I might be falling for him. Why in the hell was that thought in my brain? I'd known him for all of an hour. He could be a serial killer. This was the stuff ridiculous romance novels were made of. I was a witch with a shitty romantic track record who didn't even know the real meaning of love.

"I've waited for you a long time," he said as he brushed my wild auburn curls from my face.

"That's just silly," I said breathlessly. "You know nothing about me."

"Oh, but I do. Your Aunt Hildy talked about you so often I feel like I know you."

I rolled my eyes and made a sound of disdain. "My Aunt Hildy never laid eyes on me. How would she know the first thing about me?"

"Your father."

Now I was mad. "He doesn't know me either," I snapped and tried to roll away from Mac, but he held me close. "My father took off before I was born."

"He knows you," Mac said. "And he loves you."

Mind-shattering orgasms and hearing that a man I didn't know supposedly loved me and spoke fondly of me was simply more than I could take at the moment.

"Fairy tales," I muttered as I buried my face in Mac's collarbone. "If my father was around me he would have shown himself. If he really loved me he would have let me know."

"Sometimes things are far more complicated than that. Sometimes things happen when least expected."

"Just don't tell me you're my father and we're fine," I joked as I again tried to extricate myself. Again, no go. Mac wasn't turning me loose.

"Okay." He laughed and closed his eyes. "That was disgusting and I'm not anywhere near being your father. I'm your mate."

"About that, Mac..." I started.

"Say that again," he demanded.

"Say what?"

"My name. Say my name again."

I realized I'd never said it until then. Of course I'd known him only for an hour, but... "Mac. Mac. Mac." His smile of joy made me giggle. "But seriously, I'm not a werewolf. This whole 'I'm your mate' thing doesn't fly with me."

"But you are my mate," he said as if it was a done deal. "You're mine."

"Um... nope. Clearly we work well in the sack—or on the floor—but we're going to have to date or something."

"Date?" He was incredulous.

"Yes. Date. You know, like go to dinner, make out in the back of the movie theatre, hold hands and go on walks. Stuff like that. However—full disclosure here, I'm crappy girlfriend material."

"Do we get to keep having sex?" he asked as he mulled over my proposition, ignoring the warning.

"Well, duh. Yes."

"Okay. I can do that," he said as he slapped my ass and rolled me off of him. "We'll go on a date tomorrow night. You will wear no panties and a short skirt. We will ride my motorcycle and have sex by the river." He seemed quite pleased with his agenda.

"Dude, you will not dictate how I dress. I have extremely sexy panties and I plan to wear them."

"Can I rip them off with my teeth?" he inquired with a very naughty look in his eyes.

I considered this request for two entire seconds before I agreed. "Yes, but you'll have to buy me new ones and they're not cheap."

"Deal."

Oh my Goddess, what had I gotten myself into?

Chapter 11

"That's your cat?" Mac asked as he eyed Fabio suspiciously. Fabio hissed and eyed him right back.

"Yes, and you can't eat him. If you're hungry there are frozen pizzas in the fridge," I told Mac as we entered the kitchen. Thankfully, my gifts from the Shifters I'd healed were still in the basement. I refused to re-don bloody clothing. I was now sporting a hotter than hell Stella McCartney navy mini dress. Mac was delighted there were no panties in the stash and walked closely behind me as we mounted the stairs. He was a pig in wolf's clothing.

"You don't cook?" he asked and raised an eyebrow.

"Nope. And I have no plans to learn. Is that a problem for you?" I slapped my hands on my hips and waited for some chauvinistic remark to fly from his lips.

"Nope. I have a cook already."

"Is it a female?" I shouted. He was not going to have some wolfy bimbo cooking for him if I was anywhere in the picture.

His grin of delight at my obvious jealousy almost split his face. "No. It's a man, sweetheart. You'll love him."

"I have no plans to meet him. Ever," I shot back.

"Uh huh, whatever you say." He bit down on his lip to hide his smile. "And just so you know, I don't eat cats. I don't eat other Shifters or anything magical. However, I'd be more than happy to eat you."

He had rendered me speechless—very difficult to do. He was disgusting and I kind of loved it—not that I would ever let him know. "Out," I yelled. "You're leaving now."

His laugh made me horny again, which only served to increase my anger.

"I'll pick you up tomorrow at seven."

"If you're lucky," I muttered under my breath.

With a wink and a slap on my ass he left. Leaning on the closed door, I gulped in a deep breath and blew it out slowly between my lips. Mac was going to be a huge problem.

"Heeeeee's not goood enough for you," Fabio sniffed disdainfully.

"Somebody should probably tell him that," I said as I pulled myself together and ransacked the fridge for food. Sex made me hungry. There was nothing. Crap.

"I ceeertainly hope you didn't sleeeep with him," he hissed as he attacked his sack.

"No. We definitely didn't sleep."

"Zeeelda," he whined. "You can do better than hiiiiim."

"Fabio, how do you even know that? I'm not a prize. I'm a directionless witch on probation who's never maintained a relationship in my life." I plopped down on the sofa and let my head fall to my hands.

"Youuuuu are beautiful, powerful, smaaaart and fuuuuullll of compassion. Some young man, hopefully a waaaarlock, will be lucky to haaaaave you someday."

"You forgot materialistic and selfish. You know, you sound alarmingly like a parent instead of a familiar at the moment." I gave him the evil eyeball. "Well, not either of *my* parents. My mother didn't give a shit about me no matter how hard I tried and you know about my sperm donor."

"Was it baaaad growing up with heeeer?"

I glanced over and realized he really cared. "It was what it was. Regret and wallowing in self-pity are for pussies. No offense."

"Nooone taken. From the gooossip I've heard, yourrrr sperm dooonor does care—greatly. He's just indisposed at theeeeee moment," he said quietly.

"Yeah, well, that's awesome, but doesn't really do me any good. Can you whip up some food? I'm starved."

"Cheeeeck the porch," he advised. "I thiiink you will be happy."

***

Fabio was right and he was wrong. There was definitely food on the front porch, but it came with about fifty Shifters.

Chuck and Bob were waving from the back of the crowd.

Wanda and little Bo were organizing the dishes on a long table that had been set up on the front lawn.

DeeDee was manning the grill with a bunch of other gals and the beer was flowing freely.

WTF?

"Surprise," Chuck shouted. He ambled over and trapped me in a hug that made breathing difficult.

The term bear hug came to mind. Also the unappetizing thought of him bending my aunt over a chair...

"You're having a picnic!" he bellowed with glee.

"I can see that," I replied dryly. "Who in the hell are all these people?"

"Shifters," the rabbit I'd repaired told me as he chugged a beer.

"What's your name?" I asked him.

"Roger."

"You're joking." I bit down on the inside of my cheek to keep from laughing. He couldn't seriously be named Roger Rabbit.

His eyes narrowed and his nose twitched. I was floored to realize even in his human form I could still tell he was a rabbit.

"I wouldn't joke about that," he huffed as he stomped away.

"You're making friends fast," Chuck observed with a grin.

"Yeah, I'm good like that," I muttered as I took the beer from his hand and drank. "Are there any honey badgers here?"

The entire crowd went silent and stared at me in horror. WTH? Wanda, Bo, Simon and a very handsome man hustled over.

"Oh my dear," Wanda said. "We don't mix with the badgers or the hyenas. That would be deadly, especially now."

"The badgers have put a bounty on your head for killing a fourth of their colony," Simon informed me as he gave me a quick loving hug.

"Those little bastards were trying to kill Mac and me. What was I supposed to do?"

Should I have run? No way. I did lose a fabu outfit, but the mind-blowing orgasm I got from the wolf I'd zapped and then saved had been worth it.

"She popped the bastards like ticks," Chuck proudly announced to the crowd who began to applaud loudly. The chant started softly and then grew to proportions that made me uncomfortable.

"Whis-per-er. Whis-per-er. Whis-per-er," they yelled.

"Hold on, dudes," I shouted over the unruly group. "I'm just temporary."

All the chanting stopped. That certainly shut them up.

"I mean, um... I'm not your best witch and I, ahhh..."

The shocked and sad looks on their faces made my stomach churn.

"She's thinking about it," Simon chimed in, saving me from myself. "Plus, I'm fairly sure she just did the nasty with Mac!"

The crowd went wild again for the second time in five minutes. WTF? Did Mac have a problem getting laid? I had a hard time believing that.

"She's his mate!" the mountain lion bellowed joyously. "She said he smelled good!"

Again with the screaming and cheering.

A furious and beautiful blonde came tearing forward from the back of the group. She grabbed me by the hair, yanked my head to the side and examined my neck. "He didn't mark her," she grunted with satisfaction. "He's not mated to the witch."

This situation was not working for me. At all. A ball of fury simmered in my gut. Blondie was fixing to go down. Shimmering gold fire engulfed my arms and chest. The Shifters gasped and Blondie jumped back in terror.

"If you ever put your hands on me again," I growled, "I will remove them. As in blast them off of your arms. And for your information, I am not mated because I told him I would tear his nuts off if he mated with me. We're kind of sort of dating and if you even go near him I will zap your head bald and pop your enhanced chest. It will be permanent, so I suggest you watch your skanky butt around me. Understand?"

"You're a witch," she informed me haughtily. "A witch could never keep a wolf satisfied."

"You're a wolf?"

"Yes," she crowed proudly. "I can handle his needs. Not you."

"Interesting. That's not what he said when I was sitting on his face about an hour ago."

The laughter from the peanut gallery made me grin. I took a quick bow, but Blondie screeched in fury. She growled and started to shift.

She was actually going to attack me. At *my* house? At *my* picnic? Not happening.

I pointed my fingers and zapped her mid-shift. I did warn her. She was now bald and a negative A cup.

The crowd went crazy—jumping and screaming and high-fiving like idiots.

"That was impressive," Simon congratulated me with a shit-eating grin on his cute face. "She's an evil bitch."

"I had no choice. She was going to kill me," I said, still shocked at that simple fact and that I'd just disfigured her in front of all my neighbors. My stomach felt queasy and I grabbed on to Wanda for support.

Blondie lay shrieking on the ground as the Shifters pointed and snickered.

"Don't worry, Zelda," Wanda comforted. "She's had it coming for a long time."

"Um… well."

I blew out a frustrated breath. I couldn't leave her like that. It was wrong. It felt really good in the moment, but in the long run it would kind of suck. Blondie pathetically tried to hide her hairless head and missing breasts.

"Get up," I snapped.

I might have a semblance of a heart, but I wasn't stupid. I could be a kind witch, but I would be a kind witch with huge balls. My tone was strong and my stance even stronger. Blondie crawled to her feet and kept her head bowed.

"You're a skanky ho and if you ever challenge me again, this nice new look will be permanent. Do you follow me?"

She glanced up at me with hopeful eyes and dropped to her knees. "Yes, I follow you," she whispered in shame.

"Good. Now if any of you have a cell phone and want a picture take it now because I'm going to reverse the spell."

About twenty Shifters took quick pics. The public humiliation was slightly unnecessary, but proof of what I could do when crossed might come in handy. I quickly let my healing magic emerge to the delight of the crowd and I restored Blondie to her former beauty.

"Thank you," she said.

"You're welcome, but you have to leave. I won't enjoy myself if I'm wondering if you're going to attack me from behind."

"Right," she muttered and walked glumly to her car and left.

"You are quite the alpha bitch," Roger Rabbit said admiringly. "Mac is one lucky bastard."

"Roger," I said as I swallowed my need to laugh at his name. "I am no one's bitch. I am a selfish, unstable, materialistic, magical menace."

"Yes. You are exactly what we need—what we have waited for," the handsome man with Wanda said kindly. "Hildy always promised if anything ever happened to her one even more insane, derailed, irresponsible, psychopathic and powerful would become our benefactor."

"Who are you?" I knew he was trying to compliment me by his welcoming tone, but the descriptions, while possibly true, were highly insulting.

"He's my mate, Kurt," Wanda said as she took his hand in hers. "Kurt is the alpha of the raccoons."

Their love was unmistakable and I was a little jealous. Little Bo pushed between them and his father picked him up and laid a wet one on his cheek.

"Nice to meet you," I said. "But I don't think I can stay here. I have a life back in... um, well—a life."

"I see," Kurt said. "Well, while you're here let us show our appreciation. You have already healed many and it's time to celebrate. Simon, are you and the boys ready?"

"Yes, we are!"

Simon and several other skunk shifters had set up instruments on a makeshift stage. They all sported the same black hair with a white stripe and were all as cute as Simon. I wondered if they were brothers.

And then they sang.

And they were amazeballs.

They covered everything from Nirvana to Journey. Simon was the freakin' bomb. Plate after plate loaded down with delicious food kept being placed in my hands. Fabio held court with a bunch of pre-pubescent mountain lion shifters and taught them the finer points of ball licking—by demonstrating.

Glancing around, I wondered if Mac would come back, but I couldn't find him.

"Looking for someone?" Wanda asked with a twinkle in her eye.

"Nope."

"He'll be back. He's looking for the honey badgers to negotiate your bounty."

"Oh my Goddess," I gasped and jumped to my feet. "He can't go after those bastards alone."

"Yes, he can. And he's not alone," Chuck assured me. "He'll kill them all if they come after you."

85

"In case you guys forgot, I'm quite capable of taking care of myself," I snapped, freaked out that Mac the jackass could possibly die while I was eating a hamburger.

"Yes, but he's a man," Chuck said as if that was logical.

"And an alpha," Wanda chimed in.

"And our king," Kurt added respectfully.

I'd boffed their king? That was kind of hot and at the same time crazy.

"Did Hildy have to deal with all this shit?" I wondered out loud.

They were quiet as they exchanged loaded glances.

"Spit it out," I said. "Tell me what I need to know... Please."

"Her magic kept the order in line. Without her magic, the structure has been disrupted and all hell has broken loose," Kurt said solemnly.

"So many are dying," Wanda said.

"Wait. Can I just do some voodoo and get it back in line and then go back to my... you know, um..."

"Liiiiife?" Fabio supplied unhelpfully. I didn't have much of a life, but it was better than this crap.

"Yes. My life. You're supposed to be on my side, cat."

"I aaaaaaam," he said. "Alwaaaays."

"The voodoo has to be maintained," Chuck said sadly. "Hildy was amazing at that. I miss her." His head drooped and he quickly wiped a tear from his eye.

"You loved her," I said.

"Yes, I did. Excuse me," Chuck said as he walked away into the woods.

"Will he be safe out there?" I asked.

"He can defend himself almost as well as Mac. He'll be fine," Kurt assured me. "Now enough of this sadness. This is a party."

My mind was on Mac and Chuck, but I pasted on a smile, grabbed a beer and greeted my neighbors.

***

My brain was filled with more names than I'd ever be able to remember and my tummy was full. Everyone was gone and I was glad. I couldn't take so much normal and so much happy. I'd ended up flying shifters around the yard with magic—children and adults. It was a huge hit.

The image of Roger Rabbit shrieking like a girl and grunting 'I'm the king of the world' as I jettisoned him through the air would take weeks to remove from my brain. Whatever. It was the most fun I'd had in a very long time. I was used to being chastised for using my magic, but here I was revered. Of course I was using it for the benefit of others... maybe that was okay.

"You do realize the mating bite is very pleasurable," Wanda said as she packed away the leftovers in my fridge.

"Why would you think I need that information?" I asked as I pilfered a cookie from the tray on the counter.

"Just in case it was fear of pain holding you back, I wanted you to know it's amazing." She blew out a long breath and gave me the thumbs up.

"How amazing?"

"Amazing—amazing," she said as she fanned herself.

"Wanda, I don't know Mac—at all. And he doesn't know me. I can't just mate with a wolf—or anyone for that matter. I didn't exactly grow up with good examples of loving relationships and I'm going to be alive for hundreds of years... unless the honey badgers off my ass."

"Zelda, Shifters live for hundreds of years too, just like witches."

That was something to chew on... but that didn't change the fact I didn't know the first thing about him. Did he have siblings? Did he leave the toilet seat up? Could he do it more than one time a night? Stop. No way was I seriously considering this.

"Anyhoooo, from what I understand species can't crossbreed."

The thought actually depressed me and I wondered why Mac hadn't realized this. Maybe he had skipped school too.

"Yes." Wanda nodded her head in agreement. "But that's with Shifters mating with Shifters. Witches are different. Any magical being can mate with a witch."

Maybe witches were the O negative of the voodoo world.

87

"Wanda, I appreciate the heads up, but I'm not staying. I'm pretty sure finding my aunt's killer is my mission and I'm kind of behind on that."

"I think it was the honey badgers, or maybe the hyenas, or possibly other witches," she volunteered.

"That certainly narrows it down." I rolled my eyes and grabbed another cookie I didn't need. "I need to find the badgers."

"No, Zelda. It's not safe. We can't lose you too," she stated firmly.

Did she actually care or was it because I could heal them? I suppose it didn't really matter. I was leaving, but a tiny part of me wished it was just because she liked me.

"I'm going on a date with Mac tomorrow," I told her quickly before I asked if she actually cared about me.

"Oooooohhhh," she trilled as she grabbed her purse and made her way to the front door. "Don't do anything I wouldn't do."

"Not really helpful," I told her as I followed her. "What don't you do?"

"With my mate? Nothing." She laughed and hustled out.

These Shifters were nuts.

Chapter 12

Speaking of nuts, Fabio was on my bed doing his business.

I'd spent last night after the picnic and the entire day today on Fabio's laptop studying honey badgers and hyenas. There were secret sites that pertained to Shifters and witches. Mortals thought these were jokes, but they weren't. Hiding in plain sight was the way most magical beings lived. As to why Fabio had a top of the line computer, I had no clue and decided it was in my best interest not to pursue any line of questioning.

The late afternoon sun poured through the window and I sighed with contentment. Fabio and I had attacked the leftovers from yesterday's picnic for both breakfast and lunch. I shut the computer and grinned at the thought of a *date* with Mac. What to wear? Hmmmmmmm.

"Iiiiiii think I should accompaaany you on your oouuuting," Fabio said as he took a break.

"And why would you think that?" I asked.

I went through my outfit choices with materialistic glee.

"So youuuuuu don't loooose your dignitttty with that hairy baaastard."

"Too late. Been there. Done that," I said.

Fabio moaned and slapped his little furry head with his paw.

"I'm a grownup and you are my cat. My sex life is not your concern. I want to have some fun before I get turned into a mortal."

"Baabaaa Yaaaaaga will not take your poweeeeers," he said with confidence.

"Um... I have no clue who killed Hildy and I'm sure that's what I'm supposed to do here."

"Areeee you suuure that's your task?" he asked as he pushed a pair of chocolate thigh high boots with stiletto heels at me.

"Oh my hell, those are awesome. Did you go back to Paris?"

"Miiilan."

"Nice. And no, I'm not sure that's my task, but solving the problems with the Shifters means staying and I don't stay. Anywhere. Ever."

"That breeeaaaks my heart."

"Well, get over it. You're going to have to find another witch unless I figure this clusterfuck out."

"You're myyyyyy witch. I will go mortal with youuuuuu."

"Is that possible?" I asked. What was wrong with him? Why would he do such a thing?

"I willlllll make it soooooo."

I shook my head and grinned. The little bastard was growing on me. At night he cuddled up and purred as I fell asleep. I was almost used to waking up and seeing his nut sack cleansing ritual every morning. Almost.

"You are making it more difficult for me to mow you down with a car or put you in the pound." I scratched his furry head and then finished dressing. "How do I look?" I was rocking a super short mini and an off the shoulder fitted top.

"Like my princesssssssssss." he declared. "I juuust wish you were dating a waaarlock, not a wolf. Maaaaybe you should show a littttttle lesss cleavage."

"Warlocks are losers. I wouldn't date a magic dude ever. Too self-absorbed in the bedroom," I told him as I touched up my makeup and lowed the neckline of my shirt a bit more just to piss him off.

"TMI," Fabio grunted with disgust. "TMIIIIIIIII."

"You started it."

"Truuuuue."

"Anyhoo, I guess I've got about a week till Halloween and I'm going to…"

"Ummmmm, Zeeelda," Fabio cut me off.

"Yes?"

"Tooooooday is October thirty-first."

"Right." I laughed and slipped into my boots as I readjusted my shirt. Too much boob was not my style. I was going for sexy, not hookery. "Good one, Fab."

"It issssssssss," he hissed.

I froze and felt the leftover cookies, hamburgers and coleslaw creep up my esophagus. This was not happening. "I was passed out for two weeks," I yelled. "You all told me two weeks! It can't be the thirty-first. I have another week."

"I guesssss we were kind of off on the timing. Weeeee were worried."

"Holy shit Fabio, why didn't you say anything?"

I was two seconds away from a total freak out. The kind where lots of stuff got broken and I lost my voice for a week.

"I thought youuuuuu kneeeew." He was getting as freaked as I was.

"Clearly I did not," I shrieked. "I don't want to be a mortal."

"I willll come with youuuu. I promise."

My break down stopped for a brief moment and I looked at my cat. "Can you really do that?"

"It's never been done successfully, buuuuut I willlll try," he promised.

"Wait. You could die?" Oh my Goddess, I did not deserve this stupid cat.

"Posssssssibly."

"Then no. Absolutely not. I will not allow that. Maybe I could get some kind of visitation rights or something."

I crossed my arms over my chest and stomped my foot so he would know I was serious.

"Youuuuu like meeeee." He was positively ecstatic.

"No, I don't."

"Yessssss, you dooooooo!"

He was such a pain in my ass.

"Fine," I grumbled. "I like you. Are you happy now?"

"Dooooo you loooove me?" he asked quietly.

"Don't push your luck, cat. All of this is totally unacceptable. All of you stupid idiots are making me feel things. And I *don't* feel things. It's not good for me."

"Asssssssbuckle, West Viiirginia agrees with youuuuuuuuuu."

"No, it does not," I snapped. "I have to find the badgers. I think they killed Hildy."

"I thiiiink you're riiiight."

"You do?"

"Yesssss, but you will not gooooo alone. I will come wiiith you. You willll need my magic toooooo."

"I was supposed to ride on a motorcycle and have sex by the river." I sat down on my bed and mourned the life I couldn't have.

"Youuuuu will have sex tomorrooooooww," Fabio assured me.

"You approve of that?"

"Nooooo, but I want youuu to be happpppy."

"As nice as that sounds, I'm not sure I'll be around tomorrow to do anything."

"Yessssss, Zelda. Youuuuuu willllll."

Chapter 13

"No. Not happening," Mac spat angrily as he paced my kitchen. He looked good enough to eat in his jeans, faded t-shirt and shit kickers, and he was pissed.

"If you won't help me I'll find them on my own," I informed him in a brook-no-bullshit tone. It was a stand off and it wasn't pretty. Fabio sat on the table and watched with fascination.

"You are not going after the honey badgers," he snarled.

Mac was furious and the veins on his neck stood out. He was even hotter when he was angry and I considered asking for a quickie before I died later this evening. However, I didn't think he would go for that right now.

"I don't know which part of 'I get turned into a mortal tomorrow' you don't understand, but I have to find Aunt Hildy's killer. I've never seen the hyenas around here and I highly doubt another witch killed her so I'm starting with the fucking honey badgers."

"Why don't you think it was another witch?" he demanded.

"Because they wouldn't have left a bloody mess," I yelled and then froze as something unfamiliar clicked into place in my brain.

Believe in myself. The thoughts formed and flew from my startled lips.

"Hyenas would have left bones, but the honey badgers would have eaten her. That's why there was no body," I insisted.

Oh my Goddess. My stomach lurched and my magic ramped up to a level that made me feel high. I was right. I hadn't bothered to put any pieces together until now. And now might be too late.

"Fine. I'm going with you," Mac said tightly.

"Soooo am I," Fabio added.

"Of course you are." Mac laughed without humor and glared at Fabio.

"What is your problem with my cat?" I demanded. "That mangy bastard loves me."

"Do you love him?" Mac asked.

Fabio's ears perked up and they both watched me carefully.

"Oh my hell," I sputtered. "I don't even know what love means. I don't want anyone to ask me that question again today. I have some honey badgers to destroy."

"Go change unless you can sprint in those boots," Mac instructed as he eyed my four inch heels.

"Honey, I could run a marathon in these boots. Plus, the heel alone could put an eye out."

He grinned despite himself and ran his hand through his hair in frustration. "You are definitely my girl."

"Whatever you say." I used his own ambiguous phrase on him as I headed for the door. "Let's go pop some badgers."

***

Apparently the honey badgers met at their lair at eleven every night so we had a few hours to kill. Mac insisted we do something fun before we ruined my outfit and I agreed. Fabio was bizarrely quiet, but he rarely spoke when we weren't alone.

Two people and a cat on a motorcycle was a challenge, but we made it work. Mac drove fast and I squealed with joy as the crisp night air hit my face. Fabio, on the other hand, just dug his claws into Mac's back and hissed the entire ride into town.

Main Street was deserted, but Mac was hell bent on taking me somewhere fun.

"Mac, if this is your idea of fun we're going to have some problems," I said as I dismounted the Harley and slid Fabio into my purse.

"Hush," he said as took my hand in his.

We entered the empty hardware store and made our way to the back. I was certain I heard music, but where in the hell was it coming from?

"Are you having fun yet?" he asked with a smirk.

"Um… am I supposed to be?"

"I have fun simply staring at you," he said as he ran his thumb along my jaw.

Fabio pretended to puke in my purse.

"Well, you're weird," I said as I tried to bite back my grin of delight.

"You got that right," he replied with a chuckle.

Mac opened a rusted-out door and gently pushed me through.

No freakin' way.

There was a back room to the hardware store and it housed a huge bar—with a jukebox and a buttload of happy, dancing Shifters.

I turned and squeezed Mac's hand with a giggle. "You guys really are weird."

"Again. You are correct," he said as he pulled me into the party.

"Zelda," Simon yelled as he two-stepped up a storm with a pretty skunk girl. "So happy you're here!"

I spotted Wanda, Kurt, Chuck, DeeDee, Bob and Roger and a bunch of other Shifters whose names I couldn't remember. Most sported costumes further convincing me it really was Halloween. Little Bo and several other small cuties were next to a metal tub filled with water and apples. They were bobbing and shrieking with laughter.

Depression suddenly rolled through me at the thought of leaving them, but I needed to think about it later. First I had to live through the night.

"Dance with me," Mac said as he pulled me out on the floor. The sea of Shifters parted for us and DeeDee violently banged the jukebox with her head. The fast song was immediately replaced with a slow sexy beat. Very sneaky.

Mac nodded his approval to DeeDee, who bowed her head to him, as did the rest of the crowd.

"So I hear you're the king," I said as he pulled me into his arms and began to move to the music.

"I heard that too," Mac answered as his lips grazed my ear.

I shuddered and leaned in closer. What was it about him? Was the mating bullcrap true?

"You wanna be my queen?" he whispered in my ear.

Happy chills ran down my spine and straight to my girly bits. Time to get down to business.

"Which end do you squeeze the toothpaste from?" I asked as I copped a feel of his fine ass.

"Is this a trick question?" he inquired as he returned the favor to the delight of the crowd.

"No, I'm serious."

"The bottom," he said as he pressed his very happy camper into my stomach.

I bit my lip to keep from licking him. "You passed that one. Toilet seat. Up or down?"

"We'll have two. Mine and yours."

I was sure our dance moves were getting slightly pornographic, but my brain was getting addled with lust. As far as I was concerned we were the only two people in the bar.

"Nice answer, Wolf Boy. Do you have brothers and sisters?"

"One brother. Jacob. You healed him the other day. And thank you, by the way."

"You're welcome." The sense of pride I felt was absurd, but I refused to process that nugget. "Mom and dad?"

"They passed years ago. They were wonderful."

I had nothing to add to that one. My mother had no discernable maternal instincts and my father who apparently loved me to bits was still a complete no show.

"You're lucky," I murmured, a little less horny and a little more sad.

"Your Aunt Hildy was a wonderful person. She was like a mother to Jacob and me. I think you're right about her death. We haven't been able to avenge her because her magic is gone. It's all we can do to survive at the moment."

I didn't want to hear that. It made me feel guilty... and it made me angry that I never even knew I had an awesome aunt. I stopped dancing and stepped back. "Why on earth are we at a bar dancing if everyone's life is on the line?"

Did they all have a death wish?

"Because, beautiful girl, if you don't know if there will be a tomorrow—you have to live to the fullest today."

That shut me the hell up. Did these people have it right and I'd always had it wrong? Goddess, becoming mature and rational was taking a huge toll on me. It sucked wads.

"Mac, I..."

The rest of my unformed thoughts were drowned out by terrified screaming and the sounds of flesh tearing. Mac's body tensed and his shift started automatically. In fact, most of my new friends and neighbors were going into their shift.

We had company. I wasn't going to have to find the honey badgers because they had found me... and they were led by Blondie. Son of a bitch, I should have killed her when I had the chance. Well, no time like the present.

The fighting around me escalated and it was brutal. My magic roared through my body. I quickly scanned the room for Bo and his buddies. They had shifted and were cornered by three honey badgers with death on their agenda.

Not today.

I popped the bastards and encased the kids in an impenetrable bubble. It would be a pull on my power, but it was the best I could do. Those fuckers weren't going to

97

kill children. Holy hell they were ugly—rubbery skin and frighteningly large teeth.

"*Stay with your back against the wall,*" Mac's voice bellowed in my head. "*You'll be able to see what's coming at you.*"

I scanned the crowd for him and spotted him in a showdown with eight badgers. He was vicious and magnificent.

I quickly followed his advice.

Blondie pointed me out to a particularly big, ugly badger. I was certain he was their leader and he was gunning for me.

"That's her. That's the witch," she screamed as her face contorted into something ugly and scary. "Kill her. She dies like her aunt."

Wait. Blondie'd had something to do with my aunt's death? Why?

I was concerned about the badger, but first things first.

"Beauty is as beauty does.
The Goddess shall judge us all.
But those who thrive on blood and death,
Shall be the first to take the fall."

Blondie morphed into a hideous creature with fangs and warts before she exploded and disappeared in a cloud of black smoke. It halted the badger only briefly. His eyes widened in horror and the roar that left his slimy mouth made my eyes cross.

And then everything slowed.

The badger had magic and he was using it. It was uncomfortably familiar. It was witch magic. How in the hell did he possess witch magic?

And then I saw it. It was something I would never be able to erase—not even with a lifetime of therapy. Not even with magic. It would be my nightmare for eternity. The scene played through my head like a horror movie and it was all I could do not to throw up.

The badger was proud. He wanted to show me his kill—show me my aunt's death, before he added me to his list.

It was in Hildy's kitchen where it started. Blondie and several badgers cornered her. She tried to bargain for her life, but they laughed. I watched in horror as she tried to pull up her magic but they doused her in a blue solution that rendered her impotent. After a beating that left her bloody and weak, they threw her to the floor. Two badgers held her down as Blondie stuck a huge glowing syringe in her heart.

My aunt's weeping constricted my own heart and it was difficult to breathe. They had found a tool to drain her magic from her body and they did it with sadistic pleasure. Hildy's beautiful body writhed in pain. She chanted to the Goddess for mercy—for death, but it fell on deaf ears.

Bile rose in my throat as the badger projected the gruesome scene. His beady eyes smiled at me and his teeth gnashed.

After Blondie injected my aunt's magic into the badger, they tore her apart and ate her. Sickened didn't even begin to describe what I felt. They were barbarians and they would die by my hand. Blondie's death had been kind, but that was not a mistake I would make twice.

With a quick glance around the room, I spotted Chuck and Mac tearing the heads from the attacking honey badgers. Simon, Kurt, Wanda, Bob, Roger and DeeDee weren't faring as well, but they were alive. Some of the others weren't. The pretty skunk girl Simon had been dancing with lay dead in a bloody heap on the floor.

Thankfully the children were still safe in the bubble, but honey badgers clawed at it violently. I wasn't at full power while the bubble held, but my fury displaced my slightly lessened magical capacity.

It was time for some badgers to die.

Reaching down deep into myself, I prayed to the Goddess for guidance. We were supposed to be healers and stewards of the earth. I wasn't bloodthirsty or violent—but it rose in me now. In a very short period of time I'd become attached to these people and watching them die was simply not an option.

I could stop this. I could maybe even end this. I could choose to believe in myself. And I would.

"*Zelda, on your left,*" Mac shouted as he bound across the room to me.

An acid-like burst of pain shot through my leg as a badger bit down and locked on. How did I miss him? I fought to throw him off, but he was too strong.

Panicked, I pulled for magic, but holding the bubble surrounding Bo and his friends was more of a drain than I thought.

Fuck. Me or the kids? No choice. I would not let children die on my watch.

Mac's eyes were wild and his roar made the hair on my neck stand up as he tore the badger on my leg to shreds. I watched in horrific satisfaction. He was deadly and magnificent.

For the first time in my life someone had my back. *For real* had my back.

He licked my leg and the wound began to mend together.

"Are you trying to become the new Shifter Wanker?" I laughed. It was either laugh or cry and I was not a baby. I looked down in wonder as my leg healed completely.

"*I am keeping my mate alive so she can do her job and still have sex by the river later,*" his wolf said with great satisfaction.

I giggled and rolled my eyes. "Shall we?" I asked and indicated the shit show around us.

He nodded and rubbed his huge body against mine. "*Yes. Let's.*"

Together we moved to the center of the room. The sounds of battle made me ill. It had to stop.

Fire in every color of the rainbow engulfed my upper body as I struggled to remain standing.

Mac pressed his body to mine and I used his head for balance. Flames hissed and snapped as sparkles leapt around my head and rained over me and my wolf.

My hair blew wildly and my breath came in short gasps. I'd never conjured up this much power in my life. I hoped to hell that I didn't blow the entire building up.

I narrowed my eyes and focused my thoughts. I vaguely heard gasps and shrieks as a funnel of wind erupted from the floor and gathered every honey badger in the room except one. That badger would die slowly—very slowly. The ugly fucker hung helplessly in the air, trapped by magic as he watched his colony swirl inside the violent mini tornado.

I closed my eyes and chanted as the badgers popped one by one. It was hateful, but I did it that way so they knew what was coming as they watched their own die before them.

Their leader roared and tried to undo my spell with the magic he'd torn from my aunt's body, but I was stronger. I was also more insane, unbalanced and psychotic than he was. I had a gift he didn't. I cared. I cared for all the Shifters in the room. The ones I knew the names of and the ones I didn't. I cared for my aunt—the woman who looked just like me and hadn't deserved to die.

And I cared for the wolf who wanted me to be his. This was all ridiculous and futile as I still planned to leave, but I couldn't decipher it at the moment. I needed to protect the ones who needed me and destroy the ones who wanted me dead.

It sounded like popcorn, but it was over quickly. They were dead. The badgers could no longer hurt my people. I let the bubble around the children dissolve and they ran quickly to their parents. I didn't know how many Shifters were dead and how many lived. I had business to attend to and I would heal the wounded after.

"*I will kill him,*" Mac's voice hissed in my head as he approached the floating badger.

"No," I shouted. "He's mine."

Mac turned and stared as he shifted back to human form. Then he slowly stepped aside. The shocked murmurs that erupted through the crowd made me realize

101

this was a monumental moment. The king was sharing his power—with me.

"As you wish," he said.

My heart thundered in my chest. I wouldn't have this moment if not for him. I'd be lying dead in the corner torn apart by badgers just like my aunt had been. He had saved me and made it possible for me to avenge Hildy. To process my feelings was impossible. I wasn't good at it and this really wasn't the right time.

Later. I'd deal with it later. I had work to do.

"She didn't deserve to die by your hand," I ground out as I approached the badger who wasn't quite as confident as he had been only minutes ago. "You took her magic and now I will take it back."

I felt Mac at my shoulder as I closed the gap between myself and the horrid animal that had senselessly killed my aunt. Mac's presence calmed me and he didn't try to stop me. I realized he was really going to let me fight my own battle.

My hair still tossed wildly around my head and I saw my skin glowing eerily. I felt beautiful and powerful and loved by the people surrounding me. It was an unfamiliar feeling, but it felt good.

"*She died like a coward,*" the badger spat. "*She begged for her life.*"

He laughed maniacally and drool fell from his lips. Mac's body tensed next to me and I knew it took all he had not to destroy the evil piece of shit.

"Death will be too good for you, so I think I'll leave you to my Council," I informed him calmly watching as his eyes grew wide with terror.

Mac's body relaxed beside me and an impressed chuckle from deep in his gut left his lips.

The Witch Council was famous for torture of enemies. I wasn't clear what they did and I was quite happy to leave it that way. However, the honey badger had clearly heard about their methods.

"But before I turn you over I need something back."

I punched my fist into his chest. The squishy sound was sickening, but it was the fastest and most efficient to retrieve what belonged to my family. Aunt Hildy's magic came into my blood and guts covered hand quickly and with joy. It slid up my arm and flowed into my chest. It was warm and strong. It nestled and shuddered. I could feel my aunt inside me and my eyes filled with tears.

The badger was now unconscious, but he was still alive. He hung in the air, which was where he would stay until I could call the Council to get him. We would need to discover where that syringe was and how he came to have it.

"Oh no," Wanda cried out and my heart lodged in my throat. I turned and gasped. My voice sounded strange to my ears. She held a limp Fabio in her hands and was trying to stop the flow of blood that came from his head.

"No, no, no," I screamed as I ran to her as I gently took my mangy, ball-licking cat from her shaking arms. "You will not die, you little shit. You have at least three more lives left."

Salty tears rolled down my cheeks and to my lips as he lay still and lifeless in my arms.

I quickly pulled up all the healing magic I owned and let it wash over him but I was too late. Too fucking late.

Mac eased me to the floor as I sobbed. The helplessness I felt was tearing me to shreds. I cradled Fabio to my chest and whispered to him.

"I am so sorry," I blubbered in barely coherent English. "You drove me nuts and I did consider the pound a couple of times, but I never would have really done it. And you were right. If I had balls and I could lick them, I would have—probably more than you did. You stupid cat. You made me love you and now you're dead. This is why I don't love people or animals or anything. They don't stay. Who's going to steal me clothes from Paris now? Who's going to make me pancakes? Oh Goddess, I wish I had told you when you asked. I do, you little fucker. I love you."

My sobs racked my body and I rocked my dead cat back and forth until his weight gain made rocking impossible. WTF? I was no longer holding my sweet yet inappropriate little cat.

Nope, I was holding a huge, auburn-haired naked man with eyes that matched mine.

That's when I screamed.

Chapter 14

"Oh my Goddess, cover him up," I yelled.

I shoved the huge shocked man off my lap and slapped my hands over my eyes. He was beautiful, but for some reason his naked body repelled me. I was completely grossed out.

"Somebody cover his balls. Now! I cannot look at this man's nuts or weenie or I will puke."

I stared up at the ceiling as my friends and neighbors frantically searched for something to cover his offending privates. Finally Mac draped an orange tablecloth over the man who used to be my cat. The guy looked hideous in orange with his red hair, but that was the least of my problems at the moment.

I got right up in his face. "Who the fuck are you and what did you do with my dead cat, buster?"

His smile made me blink. It was a mirror of mine. Who in the hell was he?

"Hello, Zelda. I've waited a long time to make your acquaintance."

I was bizarrely drawn to him, so I backed away. My urge was to hug him, but he made my dead cat disappear. "I want my cat back," I snapped.

He smiled and held out his hand. I refused it and he slowly dropped it back to his side.

"Tell her who you are," Mac demanded.

"You know him?" I asked. Confusion didn't begin to cover the thoughts filling my brain.

Mac squatted down next to me and wrapped his arms around me. "I've met him several times," he said to me.

"I figured it was you," Mac said to Naked Dude.

"She could do better," Naked Dude said with authority.

Why did this sound familiar? "Are you Fabio?" I asked.

"Yes," he replied, his focus totally on me. "But I'm more."

"Yeah, clearly. You're a big naked man who I do not ever want to see naked again."

The crowd of Shifters watched. Some frowned in confusion and some smiled knowingly. Goddess, I hated not being in on the secret. This sucked and needed to end now.

"You realize you can't lick your balls anymore," I told him and then dropped my head into my hands. Why was I born without a filter? Why?

The Shifters laughed and the man chuckled. "I know. I will actually miss that," he said as I looked up and grinned.

"Who are you?" I asked again.

"Zelda, I am your father."

I was unsure if I wanted to laugh, cry or smack him. This was a shitty joke and it tore at my heart, cracking it to pieces.

"What the fuck?" I shouted. "When did we start playing *Star Wars*? I don't have a father. I have a sperm donor. You are not my father. I want my cat back."

"Zelda, I can explain." The man's voice was raw and full of emotion.

I looked to Mac. "Is he telling the truth?" I whispered the question as I leaned into him for comfort.

"He is your father, but if you don't want to talk to him I'll take you away."

Turning back, I stared at the man who claimed to be my sperm donor. At least now it made sense why I couldn't look at him naked.

"Spill it." I crossed my arms over my chest and waited. The impulse to crawl over to him was enormous.

"I didn't know about you. Your mother never told me. When I found out I confronted her and she turned me into a cat. The only way I could be with you as your father was if I earned your love."

His voice was sincere and his eyes searched mine, begging for something. I groaned and let my head fall back on my shoulders.

"It took me a very long time to love you as a cat. I have no clue if I can love you as a father. Is your name really Fabio?"

"Yes. Yes, it is."

"That's kind of unfortunate," I muttered.

"Yes, well, my sister's name was Hildegard."

He did have a point. I was glad he had no hand in naming me.

"All right, Fab—dadio," I stuttered and then expelled a large sigh. "We can go slow. Really slow. You will have to wear clothes that aren't orange and I won't call you Dad until I can say it without laughing—which may be never. I will call you Fabio or Naked Dude. You will pay for therapy until I can get the visual of your white ass and nuts out of my head and you have to tell me about Aunt Hildy."

"I can do that," he said.

His eyes sparkled with hope and I felt wanted by a parent for the first time in my life. It was a heady feeling and I didn't want to trust it, but he was here and he was smiling at me.

The magic in the ransacked bar ramped up dramatically. The Shifters huddled in fear, but I just smiled. I knew she would show up eventually. It was All Hallows Eve, after all.

"Well, this is certainly a mess," Baba Yaga purred as she and her scary cronies appeared in a poof of old lady crouch smoke.

"Yep," I agreed as I hugged her tight. She had graduated from *Flashdance* attire to appalling Madonna-esque. Hundreds of black rubber bracelets covered her arms and the cone-shaped bustier that barely contained her ample breasts could put an eye out. Her skintight silver lamé pants made me gag, but I was truly happy to see her. "I have a present for you."

"Really?" she asked as she took in my nearly naked father with interest.

"Fabio, darling, I didn't think you'd be able to do it. You made her love you! Congratulations," she said happily as she flicked her pinkie and dressed him in a heinous outfit from the eighties.

My dad slash cat cringed as he glanced down at his ensemble... at least it wasn't orange. I hoped someone's cell phone had made it through the battle. I needed a blackmail picture of this.

"What sort of present do you have for me, dear?" Baba Yaga inquired.

"I have the motherfucking assmonger who murdered Aunt Hildy. He used a syringe to drain her magic before he killed her and then he put it in himself."

"Do you eat with that mouth?" she inquired dryly.

I glanced over at Mac and exchanged grins. "Yes, I do."

"And did you take her magic back?" Baba asked as she examined the vile badger with hatred.

"I did."

"Good girl. I'd suggest you be careful with it. You now possess enough power to blow up the continental U.S."

She clapped her hands with delight and I blanched. That was far more responsibility than someone like me should have. Ever.

The warlocks surrounded the hanging badger and yanked him from the air. The looks of sadistic satisfaction on their faces made my stomach roil, but the honey badger had it coming. He had a way to kill witches and take their gifts. This was very bad and tremendously deadly to my kind.

"So your next mission, if you choose to take it, will be to find the syringe, kill all the ones who created it and destroy any evidence that is left," Baba Yaga said with her back to me. "Alone."

She turned around, readjusted her dangerous knockers and continued.

"Or you could take up your aunt's job."

WTF? How was this fair? I'd done my task. I should be free to leave and go on my merry, vapid, lonely, pathetic way.

Wait...did she say choose? I had a choice? Was this a win-win?

I could say I wanted to stay here, but everyone would assume it was because I didn't want to hunt down the deadly weapon. Finding the syringe was sure to get me killed.

Think, think, think...

No one would really know I wanted to stay. I had feelings for all these idiots and I wanted to get to know my father, not to mention have sex by the river.

Shitballs. Feelings were messy and emotions were dangerous. However, when I weighed it with being alone and most likely dead, the choice was clear. I would stay. The small fact that I wanted to stay would be my secret.

Pretending to debate the merits of the choice in my head was kind of fun. Everyone in the room was on pins and needles—especially Mac. He stared at me hard, willing me to stay with him.

Inhaling through my nose and blowing the breath out loudly between my lips, I spoke. "I will stay."

The roar of joy was deafening. Shouts of glee and hugging and crying commenced. I was fist-bumped, bear-hugged and tossed around like a doll. Finally, I ended up in Mac's arms where I was kissed so thoroughly I forgot my name. My dad stepped up and put his arms out for a hug. Slowly I went to him and it felt so right and so wonderful my eyes filled with tears. Fabio turned to my wolf while I was still in his embrace.

"I was wrong," Fabio said to Mac as I tried to calm my heart and brain. "You have my blessing. However, if you hurt her I will smite your ass to hell and back."

My father shook Mac's hand and the truce was sealed.

"Noted," Mac said.

WTF?

Baba Yaga pulled me to her. I ducked so I didn't lose my left eye to her pointed hooter. "I have always believed in you. It delights me to see that you have learned to believe in yourself."

"Was that my task?" I asked, shocked it was that simple.

"Yes, the rest of what you did was your fate." She winked and kissed my cheek. "And your mate is hot!"

"He is not my mate," I insisted loudly. "We're just dating."

"Good luck with her," Baba Yaga told a delighted Mac. "She's a handful."

"I will take care of her and will defend her until my last breath," he told the most powerful witch in the world.

My insides tingled and my woowoo clenched. Baba was correct. He was freakin' hot.

"Of course you will," she said with a bit of witchy steel in her voice. "I would have never allowed her in your presence if I didn't know this to be true. Zelda, you must use your magic to protect the balance and destroy anything in the area that is deadly to our races. Capisce?"

I grinned and then I realized what she had said...Wait one cotton picking minute.

I was stuck on the first part of her sentence.

Baba Yaga knew all of this was going to happen?

With the flourish she was known for, she and her entourage disappeared in a cloud of crouch smoke before I was able to ask another question or demand answers.

"You realize she kind of screwed you over," Simon said as he and Chuck began to clean up the carnage.

"What are you talking about?" I was still shocked by the events of the evening—mostly that this was my new home. "Don't clean up. I'll use some magic to clear out the shit show."

"You've done enough tonight," Fabio cut in. "Allow me."

With a flick of his hand, silver and gold sparkling mist covered the room. Everything was returned to its former glory and all the blood and carnage disappeared. My dad had some awesome magic. I hoped he would still make me pancakes and steal fantabulous designer duds for me... time would tell.

I was delighted to realize I was wrong about Simon's skunk girlfriend. She wasn't dead, but she was badly injured. I had work to do. Amazingly none of the Shifters had died. I silently thanked the Goddess for my beautiful healing gift.

"Line all the wounded up. Do it fast before I change my mind and go after the fucking syringe," I told the crowd.

"Did you not take in what I just said?" Simon asked as he helped his girlfriend to the line.

"Nope. Explain," I said as I began to heal a mangled fox.

"Baba Yaga," he started.

"Call her Booby Yumpy," I corrected him, then I winced in pain as the fox's cracked skull mended. I quickly blasted and swore my way through the rest of the wounded. Which left only Chuck with a large tear in his belly.

"Nice work." Simon grinned. "Booby Yumpy really gave you no choice at all."

"How's that?" I grunted as I fixed the bloody hole in Chuck's stomach.

"She told you to protect the area. She told you to maintain the balance and destroy anything in the area that threatened our races."

"Yes. And?"

This cryptic shit was giving me more of a headache than healing head wounds.

"Spit it out," I demanded.

"The syringe is in the area. It will be your responsibility to find it and eliminate it," Simon said as he backed away.

My magic turned from lavender to green and began to shoot erratically around the room. Shifters ducked for cover.

"That is so fucking unfair," I shouted. "She is such a bitch. So I had no choice at all. I'm going to die finding the syringe."

"You will not die because you will not be fighting alone—ever again," Mac said with authority.

"You heard her," I snapped. "I have to do it by myself."

"No. That was the first choice. You rejected the first choice. You chose to stay. You have a very large extended family now who will have your back."

His eyes were warm and filled with something I was afraid to name.

I calmed and peeked around the room. Shifters nodded and stood tall. I was amazed and humbled. How did this happen to me?

"I will defend you and help you," Fabio said as he dropped to his knee.

"So will I," Chuck and Simon called out and then knelt down like my father.

They started an avalanche of shouting. Every single Shifter in the room called out their support and then went down on bended knee. Mac stood beside me and took it all in.

"You are loved," he whispered.

I wanted to ask him if he meant by him, but I wasn't ready to have the tables turned back on me. Raw emotion was tricky and I wasn't sure I knew what love really meant… yet.

But just maybe I was willing to try.

"Can we still go to the river?" I asked shyly.

"Would you like that?" he asked with a twinkle in his eye.

"Would you?" I countered.

"More than anything in the world," he assured me as the crowd cheered. It was a little disconcerting to know we were getting whoops and whistles for going off to have sex in a public area, but I didn't care. I wanted this man more than I wanted the new Prada bag that wasn't on the market yet.

"We can't mate yet," I told him seriously.

"Yet?" His joyous smirk made me giggle. "There's a chance for me?"

"Possibly, but you have to pass some more tests and take me out on fifteen dates where no one dies. Deal?"

"Deal."

His kiss was downright lewd. I wrapped my legs around him as he carried me out of the bar and into the cold Halloween night. I said goodbye to no one. I couldn't see anything except the strong, beautiful man in front of me. We would definitely have fights if we were mated. I could feel it in my gut, but we would also have joy and some of the greatest sex ever.

"Would I really have puppies?" I asked.

He stopped and chuckled.

"No, Zelda. We will have human babies, but they will be very special. They will be Shifters with healing magic."

"Did you say babies?"

His sexy grin melted me. "Yep."

"I'm agreeing to nothing," I snapped as he plopped me on his motorcycle. "I'm just on a fact finding mission."

"Whatever you say." His voice was gruff and my panties dampened.

"Just get on the bike and drive," I said as I punched him and he threw his head back and laughed. "*Now.*"

I was seconds from jumping his fine ass in the parking lot. We needed to get to the river immediately.

"Will do, my love. Will do."

Epilogue

Dear Aunt Hildy,

I know it's a little odd to write to you considering you're dead and I have no clue if you will ever see this, but I wanted to put down in words what I wish I could say to you.

I would have loved to have known you. Watching the replay of your death was one of the worst moments of my life. I want you to know that I got the fucker who killed you and took your magic. He's with the Warlock Council. I am sure he has wished for death many times over. Those old bastards are scary.

I took your magic back and it's inside me. It comforts me to know I possess part of you. I would much prefer to have you with me, but if this is the way it was meant to be just know I will take good care of it and do my best not to blow up the continental U.S. However, I can't promise that I can control that.

Most of this adventure has been a clusterfuck, but I am still alive to tell. I found my father, your brother, and I'm dating Mac. I thought you might like to know that. As far as Fabio, or "Naked Dude" as I like to call him goes, we are taking it slow. He likes to shop for me and he makes outstanding pancakes. He misses licking his balls, but I'm sure anyone would. I'm beginning to think we can make the family thing work. I can't seem to bring myself to call him Dad, but he seems to be getting used to "Naked Dude".

I plan to stay in Assjacket, West Virginia for the time being. I think I'm happy which scares the hell out of me, but I want to give it a chance. Mac thinks I'm his mate, but he still has fourteen death-free dates to go before I will give his claim any serious consideration. He has sworn repeatedly that we would not have puppies, but I am still searching for proof.

I've made real friends here and I'm proud of the way I use my magic. I refuse to share these facts with anyone but you because you're dead and real emotion is uncharted territory for me. I'm not ready to go there yet.

I promise to take care of the Shifters. I am going by Shifter Wanker, not Shifter Whisperer. It's a long story, but trust me, the name suits. I will find that fucking syringe and I will destroy it. I so wish you were here to help me, but I know that's impossible. Even though I didn't know you I miss you terribly. Thank you for the beautiful home. However, I wish you were a size four because you had rockin' taste in clothes.

I did get a TV. Actually "Naked Dude" probably bought it with bad credit cards. I can't believe you lived without one. I would love to watch Project Runway with you. Or Spongebob. Regrets are for pussies and I am not a pussy. I send you my love and hope you are in a beautiful place. I will cherish our home and keep your spirit alive.

Currently '"Naked Dude" is soundproofing his bedroom. Apparently Mac and I are loud.

xoxo Zelda (the Shifter Wanker)

I flicked my finger and a burst of icy pink and silver crystals flew through the room. I grinned. It was Hildy's magic. I'd gained colors I never knew existed. A sparkling mystical breeze picked up the note and with another flick of my hand the note magically disappeared into the universe. There was no telling if it would fall into Aunt Hildy's hands, but for some bizarre reason... I thought it just might.

THE END (for now)
###

Note From the Author

If you enjoyed this book, please consider leaving a positive review or rating on the site where you purchased it. Reader reviews help my books continue to be valued by distributors and resellers, and help new readers make decisions about reading them. You are the reason I write these stories and I sincerely appreciate you!

Many thanks for your support,
~ Robyn Peterman

Visit my website at www.robynpeteman.com.

Book Lists (in correct reading order)

HOT DAMNED SERIES

Fashionably Dead
Fashionably Dead Down Under
Hell on Heels
Fashionably Dead in Diapers
Fashionably Hotter Than Hell

SHIFT HAPPENS SERIES

Ready to Were
Some Were in Time

MAGIC AND MAYHEM SERIES

Switching Hour
Witch Glitch

HANDCUFFS AND HAPPILY EVER AFTERS SERIES

How Hard Can it Be?
Size Matters
Cop a Feel

If after reading all the above you are still wanting more adventure and zany fun, read Pirate Dave and His Randy Adventures, the romance novel budding novelist Rena was helping wicked Evangeline write in How Hard Can It Be?

Warning: Pirate Dave Contains Romance Satire, Spoofing, and Pirates with Two Pork Swords.

Excerpt from WITCH GLITCH

Magic and Mayhem, Book 2

Chapter 1

"What in the hell does that asswaffle think he's doing?" I snapped as I narrowed my eyes at the scene unfolding on the beautiful front lawn of my newly inherited house.

Crawling up onto the window seat I pressed my face against the glass to make sure I was seeing things correctly...unfortunately, I was.

Chuck the ginormous bear Shifter had concocted a noose and was trying to hang himself in a large tree. This was not going to happen in my yard. Dead stuff smelled horrific and I had an over active gag reflex as did most witches I knew.

Opening the widow with a pissed off blast of magic, I leaned out and prepared to zap his idiot ass. As the newly minted town Shifter Whisperer--or Shifter Wanker as I liked to refer to my job, I wasn't about to heal a self-inflicted broken neck.

"Chuck, what in the Goddess' name do you think you're doing?" I shouted as he fell off the ladder he was standing on and plopped ungracefully to the ground with a thud.

"Well, I was trying to hang myself until you scared the bejesus out of me," he explained logically as if what he was doing was even remotely logical.

"Well, ok, but you're going to have to take your freak show to someone else's tree. I have a lot of shit to do today and watching you die is not on my list."

"But I have to do it here," he informed me as he ambled up to the porch.

"I am about to ask a question I have no desire to know the answer to--but why?"

Shifters were the weirdest species ever. I had always thought witches were nuts. We had nothing on the Shifters.

"I can't tell you," he mumbled into his shoulder.

He was a beautiful and kind man and I liked him, which annoyed me. I was getting far too attached to the oddballs in Assjacket, West Virginia. I had chosen to stay after I had paid my penance to the Witch Council, but if these dorks were going to pull stunts like hanging themselves in my trees I was out of here.

"I call bullshit," I snapped. "You can't just off yourself in someone's Silver Oak and not tell them why. It's rude."

"I'm sorry, Zelda," he apologized as he rocked back and forth in embarrassment. "If I could tell you I would. I just can't break the rules. I could end up naked and wedged in a time warp with elevator music."

"You lost me," I said as I reconsidered zapping his ass just for making my brain work too hard at 8AM in the morning.

"It's no big deal. I can try again another time when you're out shopping. I'll just be on my way," he said with a smile.

I really wanted to shut the window and pretend I hadn't just seen the dumbass try to end his life, but my newly found conscience wasn't on the same page. Biting down hard on my tongue, I attempted to keep my words from flying out of my mouth--no fucking go. Apparently speak first and think later was my new motto.

Damn it.

"Chuck, um...emotions and being nice are not really my thing, but I'm feeling kind of wonky here. Are you depressed? Can I heal that?" I asked as mentally slapped myself for caring.

"Actually, I'm not down at all," he replied with a shrug and a happy little grunt. "I'm quite content, but thank you for your concern."

"Ooookay then, you should probably take the ladder and rope with you then," I mumbled not quite sure what was socially acceptable to say in a situation like this.

"Can I just leave them here for next time?"

"Um, no. You can't."

"Alrighty," he said as he gathered up his death tools and loaded them into his truck. "Oh and by the way, when I do bite it I'd like you to have my truck."

"Really?" I squealed with excitement and then purposely banged my head against the windowsill. It was a kick ass truck, but I'd rather win it in a poker game than inherit it due to his death. "Absolutely not," I hissed to cover my wildly inappropriate reaction. "You are not going to die. I will kill you if you do."

"Would you?" he asked hopefully.

"Would I what?" I rolled my eyes in exasperation.

"Kill me?"

"Holy shitballs, I wasn't serious," I shouted. "I'm the freakin' Shifter Wanker. I heal you furry jackasses, not kill you."

"Right," he said with a nod and a grin. "My bad."

"I should say so," I muttered as I closed the window and flopped down on the cushy couch. This day was going to be a long one...I could feel it in my bones.

"Zelda?" a loud voice boomed from the kitchen. "Do you want French toast or pancakes?"

I heaved a put upon sigh and stood up. "French toast would be a nice change, Naked Dude. And where are all the groceries coming from? Are you using bad credit cards again?"

"I really wish you would call me dad," Naked Dude said as he stuck his head out from the kitchen. "I'm not naked you know."

He was correct. He wasn't naked. However, he *was* buck-ass naked when I made his acquaintance only a few weeks before. It had been traumatic and repulsive. No one should have to see their father's nads. Ever. Not to mention he'd been my cat for two years...As the story goes, he never knew about me. When he found out he had a daughter he tried to contact me and my not so motherly mother had put a spell on him that turned him into a mangy cat. That mangy cat had become my familiar much to my disgust. The spell could only be broken if he gained my love.

Of course it took him almost dying for me to admit I loved him. Now we were trying to get to know each other. It was challenging and somewhat amazing, not that I would admit that to him. I'd always thought he didn't want me--at least that's what my mother had told me. The relief I felt when I learned he never knew about me was absurd so I mostly ignored it. I wasn't real good at maintaining relationships, but I was going to try.

"Look, I could drop the Naked and just call you Dude. Would that help?" I bargained.

His grin was infectious and his sparkling green eyes matched my own. "It's a start."

"I could call you Fabio. That *is* your name," I added as I sat down and dug in. I'd broach the bad credit card issue after my stomach was full.

"I'd really like you to try dad," he said as he added two more pieces of French toast to my plate.

Thank the Goddess witches had crazy fast metabolism or I'd be the size of a house. Eating was my favorite hobby and Naked Dude could cook.

"And I'd really like the Prada bag that isn't out yet," I shot back.

"Not a problem," Naked Dude/Fabio/ Dad said with a sly grin on his ridiculously handsome face.

My dad, for lack of a better word, liked to buy/steal me designer duds and accessories. This was a bad thing. I knew it was a bad thing. It was a terrible bad illegal thing. However, his logic that he also used his questionable credit cards to give tens of thousands to charity made me feel a little better about keeping my dubious booty.

"You can do that?" I asked as I poured an obscene amount of syrup on the mountain of French toast.

"I can transport to Milan, buy the bag and be back in an hour or two," he told me as he took the sugary goo from my hands before I could drain the bottle.

"*Buy* being the operative word..."

"But of course," he replied with an innocent look that probably worked on most people except me.

"But I would have to call you dad..." I pondered aloud.

"That's the deal."

I considered it.

I'm ashamed to say I really did.

"I'm not there yet, Naked Dude...I mean Dude. As much as it pains me to say no to the bag--and it does pain me, I'm just not ready to take that step."

"I understand," he said as he lovingly tucked some of my wild red locks that mirrored his behind my ear. "I'll just get the bag and keep it in my closet until you're ready."

"That's unacceptable not to mention blackmail," I said as I slapped his hand away and tried to bite back my giggle. "You totally suck."

"I know." He gave me a lopsided grin and transported to Milan in a cloud of silver smoke.

"What a dick," I mumbled to no one since I was finally alone.

My year had been an interesting one. I'd spent nine months in the magic pokey for killing my cat who miraculously rose from the dead and turned out to be my father. To be fair to me, it had been an accident. When I heard the first crunch I'd freaked out so much that I hit reverse and drive a few times before I got out of my car and screamed bloody murder. I buried him in a new Prada shoebox and left the super soft shoe bags inside as a blanket and a pillow. After Naked Dude's resurrection, he'd complimented me on his cozy coffin.

Of course, it didn't matter to Baba Yaga, the most powerful and horrendously dressed witch in existence, that it had been an accident or that my cat/dad had actually lived. I had to serve time with a heinous cellmate named Sassy the Violent Witch From Hell--as I enjoyed referring to her. Not that she enjoyed it so much, but annoying her had helped pass the time. When released, I found out I had an aunt that had left me her house--a dead aunt that I never knew. My mission ended up being avenging her, taking over her job as the Shifter Whisper and maintaining the magical balance in Assjacket, West Virginia. I had no clue what Sassy's mission had been, I was just delighted to be rid of her.

It hurt like a mother fucker to heal the random wounds of all the idiot Shifters in town, but secretly I kind of liked my new job--not the pain--the job. I'd never stayed anywhere very long and had few friends to show for it. Sassy did not count. Belonging somewhere was new to me and it felt nice. However, I refused to get used to it. I was a survivor and had gone most of my life as a loner. Less messy that way.

I suppose the best thing about Assjacket was Mac. The redonkulously hot wolf Shifter that mistakenly thought I was his mate...

Speaking of hot asses, broad shoulders and outstanding lip locking, I had a lunch date with the wolf this afternoon.

Maybe today wouldn't turn out as badly as it had begun.

Chapter Two

"How do I look?" I asked Naked Dude as I twirled around in my rockin' Alice and Olivia mini dress with my hot pink combat boots and cashmere shrug.

"Nice I suppose," he replied cautiously.

Naked Dude was never one to hold back an opinion and his reticence pissed me off. He'd been back from Milan for an hour and it took everything I had not to ransack his closet for the Prada bag.

"Suppose?" I asked with narrowed eyes as green sparks began fly from my fingertips.

"It's not the outfit." He sighed dramatically, yet backed away from the impending fireworks. "It's the company you're keeping."

"I thought you approved of Mac."

"He's tolerable for a wolf, but it really would be wonderful if you'd meet a nice stable warlock and settle down--have a few witch babies and make me a grandwarlock," he explained as he handed me a fork and a bowl of raw cookie dough to snack on.

"This is exactly why I can't call you dad," I informed him with a mouthful. "You're delusional. There is no such thing as a nice stable warlock. You are the most stable warlock I have ever met and you're certifiable."

"Thank you...I think."

"It wasn't a compliment, Na...Dudio. And let me just add that I am no prize."

"Of course you are," he interrupted. "You're beautiful, smart, powerful, compassionate, kind, and you're a wonderful eater."

"Have you been living here?" I shouted. "Sure I might be hot and powerful and can eat like a horse, but I am not kind or compassionate. I have never maintained any sort of relationship in my entire life and Mac still likes me. Plus his ass is outstanding."

My father heaved a huge sigh and pilfered some of the pre-lunch cookie dough. I considered stabbing his hand with my fork but that seemed like a little much. I settled for flicking some dough at his forehead.

"Zelda, you sell yourself short," he said as he absently wiped the goop away and licked it from his fingers.

"Oh my Goddess, you just put my spit in your mouth." I shuddered and scrunched my face in disgust.

"Not following you," Dude said in confusion.

"You ate the dough off of your face."

"Yes. And?"

"It came from the fork--which by the way was a weird utensil to hand me to eat dough--that had been in my mouth. Therefore, it stands to reason that some of my saliva was on the fork and most likely the dough that you just ate," I explained.

"So?"

"So you just swallowed my spit. That's gross."

"Zelda, I missed your entire growing up. I never changed your diaper, got spit up on or vomited on by you. I think I'm due a little spit here and there," he said with a wink and a shrug.

I was silent as I shoved more cookie dough in my mouth and wondered why I felt like crying. Naked Dude sat silently and watched. In my weirdly magnanimous mood I offered him some dough off my saliva fork and he gratefully accepted. I watched his Adam's apple bob as he swallowed the raw sugar and spit. Dropping my head into my hands I groaned.

"You're not playing fair. All that stuff about poop and pee and puke is kind of beautifully horrifying," I mumbled through my fingers.

"I'm good that way," Dude said with a gentle smile. "I missed a lot. I can't make up for not being there for you and I can't say I want to slurp spit on a regular basis, but I would die for you. I fell in love with you the very first day you found me in the dumpster."

"You were kind of hard to avoid," I said as I remembered trying like hell to keep walking past the pitiful mewing on that fated day.

For some unknown reason I stopped and peeked. He was the most mangy and stinky little fur ball of a cat I'd ever seen. I was repulsed by him, but shockingly it didn't stop me from saving his feline ass. Of course I regretted it daily for the two years he'd followed me around like a deranged shadow and drove me nuts, but now it made more sense.

I suppose I'd seen myself in the odiferous dumpster diver...starved for affection and totally alone.

Introspective though was not my forte so I shoved that profound little nugget to the recesses of my brain. This getting to know you crap was becoming messy. I didn't do messy. However, there were some things I wanted to know...

"Did you love my mom?" I asked.

It was a question I'd always pondered. My mom was not very lovable. I loved her--kind of. It was more of a perfunctory thing. All creatures were supposed to love their mothers. However, if the mother didn't love the creature back it became an exercise in futility and a need for therapy as an adult.

Naked Dude put his elbows on the table and put his chin on his palms as he clearly fought for a way to tell me he didn't love her. The thought depressed me, but I expected no less.

"I thought I did," he said quietly. "I didn't know her very well when we started seeing each other."

"You mean screwing each other," I supplied.

No time or need to mince words here.

"Well...um, yes. That would be one way to put it."

"So you did her and left?"

128

"Not exactly," he hedged. "I honestly didn't know her name the first several times."

I gaped in horror. "You're a total man whore."

"*Was*," he corrected. "I *was* a total man whore. Now I'm simply a warlock who misses licking his balls."

I closed my eyes and pinched the bridge of my nose. The visual he'd just conjured up threatened the contents of my stomach. When he'd been my cat he had an unhealthy obsession with cleaning his nut sack. Clearly it was still an issue.

"Alright, let's get back on track here," I muttered. "You nailed her a few times. She got pregnant and you left?"

"Nope."

"Enlighten me," I snapped.

As much as I wanted to keep the past in the past...I needed to know.

"Apparently I wasn't the only one *nailing* her. I left when I found out I was one of many," he supplied with a shrug.

"How many?"

"You really want to know?" he asked with a grimace.

"Do I?"

"I'd say no."

"Oh fuck, now I have to know. Let me guess. Tell me if I'm hot or cold," I said. "Four."

"Frigid."

"Eight?"

"Very cold."

"Holy shit...um, twelve?"

"Shivering."

"Mother fucker...pun intended...twenty five?"

"Cool-ish"

He was correct. I really didn't want to know, but I'd come this far. I wasn't a quitter. And apparently neither was my mother.

"Is it an odd or even number?" I asked needing to narrow the field a little. I was truly on the verge of getting sick.

"It's an odd number ending in five and is ten higher than your last guess," Dude said ending the game before I projectile hurled on him.

"Wait," I said as the circus in my stomach went ballistic. "How do I know you're actually my sperm donor? It could be one of thirty-five," I choked out.

This was not fair. This guy had found me and told me he was my dad. Told me he loved me...and as much as I had no intention of admitting it, he was growing on me. My head spun and my vision narrowed.

"Look at me," Dude demanded as I gulped for air. "Now."

I glanced up from my panic attack and saw a mirror image of myself. It was certainly hard to deny I was his by looks...

My heart slowly stopped hammering in my chest and my breathing returned to normal. I was his. I didn't want to deal with the fact of how happy that made me so I settled for a small smile and a nod.

"You are from a very powerful line of witches. Only our line has red hair and can heal," he said as he took my shaking hand firmly in his. "Our responsibility to our race and others is rather large--and somewhat overwhelming. You should have been trained since the time you were a child, but I didn't know...I didn't know you were out there."

"Wait. You're a healer too?" I asked.

"Yes, but the witches in our line are far more powerful than the warlocks."

"So I could kick your ass?" I asked as a smirk pulled at my lips.

"Yes. Yes you could."

Naked Dude chuckled and pulled me close. It felt nice so I let him. Getting used to this sappy shit was dangerous. However, living on the edge was another one of my mottos.

"Are you going to train me?"

"My sister Hildy would have been so much better, but I will have to suffice."

"I'm not a very good student," I admitted as I disengaged myself and dove back into the cookie dough before I asked him if I could cuddle up on his lap.

"You'll be fine. You've already proven your heart by selflessly healing and defending the Shifters. Controlling the magic is what you need to work on. You have the potential to blow up the continental USA."

My stomach lurched. No one needed that much power and a loose cannon like me had no business possessing that kind of magic. Whatever. It was what it was.

"I should probably change my name to Walking Time Bomb," I mused as I picked the chocolate chips out of the batter. I knew I should stop stuffing my face. I was going to lunch with Mac, but eating kept me from revealing too much of myself to Naked Dude.

"You are no such thing," he chided. "That title belongs to your mother."

"Here's something I don't understand--at your age and with your level of magic, I'm not clear how she was able to put a spell on you. You are one powerful mother humper," I told him.

"Literally or figuratively?" he inquired with a raised eyebrow.

It took me a moment, but when I got it I grinned like an idiot.

"Both, I suppose."

Naked Dude considered his answer. His knee bounced and I could literally feel him wracking his brain to come up with an answer that would satisfy me.

"No lies," I insisted.

His head dropped to his chest and he shook it from side to side. He heaved a sigh and then stared at the ceiling.

"She said she would harm you unless I dropped my magic and let her do what she wanted."

"She harmed me my whole life," I countered. "Mostly emotionally."

"She never killed you," he replied woodenly.

That certainly shut me the hell up. I mentally calculated how much fucking therapy it was going to take to get rid of the lovely knowledge that my own mother had threatened to kill me.

"Well, that's fanfuckingtastic," I said with a hollow laugh. "Would she have done it?"

"Honestly, I don't know," Dude admitted. "I was not going to take that chance. You're my daughter."

"So you let her turn you into a cat?"

"I wouldn't say *let*...I had no clue what she was going to do," he said as he stood and removed the now empty bowl in front of me.

"Oh my Goddess. She could have killed you."

The small bit of feeling I had for my mother had now evaporated. She was a monster. Wrapping my brain around the fact that Fabio would have willingly died for me was more than I could handle. It made me happy, sad and furious all at once. The burning in my gut raced throughout my trembling body.

The tablecloth was on fire before I even knew what had happened.

"Shitballs," I shrieked.

Thankfully Naked Dude was one step ahead and doused the flames with a flick of his hand.

I really *didn't* have control of my magic. Fury was going to either get us all killed or burn my house down.

"Sorry," I mumbled as I quickly sat on my hands. "We should probably start my lessons soon. Like yesterday."

"We will start tomorrow. I'll tell you all about your Aunt Hildy and we will figure out how to keep you from being a magical menace," Dude said.

"Do you think the world will be safe from me till then?"

"I certainly hope so. I have a yoga lesson at five."

"Um...that's just weird."

"You think me doing yoga is weird after everything we've just talked about?" he asked as he washed the bowl and placed it in the dishwasher.

"Yep, I do."

"My kid says the darndest things," he replied with a delighted smile.

"Oh my Goddess." I groaned and giggled. "You loved saying that, didn't you?"
"Yes. Yes I did."

Excerpt from FASHIONABLY DEAD
Book 1 in the Hot Damned Series

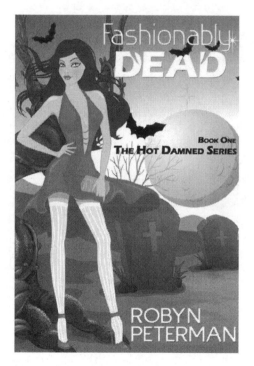

Snarky, Sexy Vampire Fun!

Prologue

I drew hard on the cigarette and narrowed my eyes at the landscape before me. Graves, tombstones, crypts...she didn't belong here. Hell, I didn't belong here. My eyes were dry. I'd cried so much there was nothing left. I exhaled and watched as the blue grey smoke wafted out over the plastic flowers decorating the headstones.

Five minutes. I just needed five minutes and then I could go back...

"That's really gross," Gemma said, as she rounded the corner of the mausoleum I was hiding behind and scared the hell out of me. She fanned the smoke away and eyed me. "She wanted you to quit, maybe now would be a good time."

"Agreed. It's totally gross and disgusting and I'm going to quit, regardless of the fact that other than you, Marlboro Lights are my best friend...but today is definitely not the day," I sighed and took another long drag.

"That's pathetic," she chuckled.

"Correct. Do you have perfume and gum?"

"Yep." She dug through her purse and handed me a delicate bottle.

"I can't use this. It's the expensive French shit."

"Go for it," she grinned. "You're gonna need it. You smell like an ashtray and your mother is inside scaring people to death."

"Son of a..." I moaned and quickly spritzed myself. "I thought she left. She didn't want to come in the first place."

"Could have fooled me," Gemma said sarcastically, handing over a piece of gum and shoving me from my hiding place.

"Come on," I muttered, as my bossy best friend pushed me back to my beloved grandmother's funeral.

***

The hall was filled with people. Foldout tables lined the walls and groaned under the weight of casseroles, cakes and cookies. Men and women, most of whom I knew, milled around and ate while they gossiped. Southern funerals were a time to socialize and eat. A lot.

As I made my way through the crowd and accepted condolences, I got an earful of information I could have happily lived without. I learned that Donna Madden was cheating on her husband Greg, Candy Pucker had gained thirty pounds from eating Girl Scout cookies and had shoved her fat ass into a heinous sequined gown, *for the funeral no less,* and Sam Boomaster, the Mayor, was now a homosexual. Hell, I just wanted to leave, but I had to find my mother before she did something awful.

"I loved her." Charlie stopped me in my tracks and grabbed my hand in his old gnarled one.

His toupee was angled to the left and his black socks and sandals peeked out from his high-water plaid pants. He was beautiful.

"Me too," I smiled.

"You know I tried to court her back in the day, but she only had eyes for your Grandpa." He smoothed his sweater vest and laid a wet one on my cheek...and if I'm not mistaken, *and I'm not,* he grabbed my ass.

"Charlie, if you touch my butt again, I'll remove your hand." I grinned and adjusted his toupee. He was a regular in the art class I taught at the senior center and his wandering hands were infamous.

"Can't blame a guy for trying. You have a nice ass there, Astrid! You look like one of them there supermodels! Gonna make some lucky man very happy one day," he explained seriously.

"With my ass?"

"Well now, your bosom is nothing to scoff at either and your legs..." he started.

"Charlie, I'm gonna cut you off before you wax poetic about things that will get you arrested for indecency."

"Good thinking, girlie!" he laughed. "If you ever want to hear stories about your Nana from when we were young, I'd be happy to share."

"Thanks, Charlie, I'd like that."

I gave him a squeeze, holding his hands firmly to his sides and made my way back into the fray.

As I scanned the crowd for my mother, my stomach clenched. After everything I had to put up with today, the evil approaching was just too much. Martha and Jane, the ancient matriarchs of the town and the nastiest gossips that ever lived were headed straight for me. Fuck.

"I suppose you'll get an inheritance," Jane snapped as she looked me up and down. "You'll run through it like water."

"Your Nana, God bless her, was blind as a bat when it came to you," Martha added caustically. "I mean, my God, what are you? Thirty and unmarried? It's just downright disrespectable."

"I'm twenty-nine, happily single and getting it on a regular basis," I said, enjoying the way their thin lips hung open in an impressive O.

"Well, I've never," Jane gasped.

"Clearly. You should try it sometime. I understand Mr. Smith is so vision impaired, you might have a shot there."

Their appalled shrieks were music to my ears and I quickly made my escape. Nana would have been a bit disappointed with my behavior, but she was gone.

Time to find the reason I came back in here for...I smelled her before I saw her. A waft of Chanel perfume made the lead ball in my stomach grow heavier. I took a deep breath, straightened my very vintage Prada sheath that I paid too much for, plastered a smile on my face, said a quick prayer and went in to the battle.

"Mother, is everything alright?"

She stood there mutely and stared. She was dressed to the nines. She didn't belong here...in this town, in this state, in my life.

"I'm sorry, are you speaking to me?" she asked. Shit, she was perfect...on the outside. Gorgeous and put together to a degree I didn't even aspire to. On the inside she was a snake.

"Um, yes. I asked you if..." I stammered.

"I heard you," she countered smoothly. "If you can't bother to comply with my wishes, I can't be bothered to answer you."

"Right," I muttered and wished the floor would open and swallow me. "I'm sorry, I meant Petra. Petra, is everything alright?"

"No, everything is not alright," she hissed. "I have a plane to catch and I have no more time or patience to make chit chat with backward rednecks. It was wrong of you to ask me to be here."

"Your mother died," I said flatly. "This is her funeral and these people are here to pay their respects."

"Oh for God's sake, she was old and lived well past her time."

I was speechless. Rare for me, but if anyone was capable of shocking me to silence, it was my mother.

"So, like I said, I have a plane to catch. I'll be back next week." She eyed me critically, grimacing at what she saw. "You need some lipstick. You're lucky you got blessed with good genes because you certainly don't do anything to help."

With that loving little nugget, she turned on her stiletto heel and left. I glanced around to see if we'd been overheard and was mortified to see we had clearly been the center of attention.

"Jesus, she's mean," Gemma said, pulling me away from prying eyes and big ears.

"Do I look awful?" I whispered, feeling the heat crawl up my neck as the mourners looked on with pity. Not for my loss, but for my parentage.

"You're beautiful," Gemma said. "Inside and out."

"I need to smoke," I mumbled. "Can we leave yet?"

Gemma checked her watch. "Yep, we're out of here."

"I don't want to go home yet," I said, looking around for Bobby Joe Gimble, the funeral director. Where in the hell was he and did I need to tip him? Shit, I had no clue what funeral etiquette was. "Do I have to...?"

"Already took care of everything," Gemma told me. "Let's go."

"Where to?" I asked. Damn, I was grateful she was mine.

"Hattie's."

"Thank you, Jesus."

***

Hattie's sold one thing and one thing only. Ice cream. Homemade, full of fat, heart attack inducing ice cream. It was probably my favorite place in the world.

"I'll have a triple black raspberry chip in a cone cup," I said as I eyed all the flavors. I didn't know why I even looked at them. I was totally loyal to my black raspberry chip. My ice cream couldn't talk back to me, break up with me or make me feel bad. Of course, my love could extend the size of my ass, but I wasn't even remotely concerned about that today. Besides, I planned a very long run for later. I needed to clear my head and be alone.

"Sorry about your loss, Sugar," Hattie said and I nodded. Her big fleshy arms wobbled as she scooped out my treat. "Do you want sprinkles and whipped cream on that, Baby?"

"Um..." I glanced over at Gemma who grinned and gave me a thumbs up. "Yes, yes I do."

"Me too," Gemma added, "but I want mint chip, please."

"You got it, Sugar Buns," Hattie said and handed me a monstrous amount of ice cream. "It's on me today, Astrid. I feel just terrible I couldn't be at the funeral."

"That's okay, Hattie. You and Nana were such good friends. I want your memories to be of that."

"Thank you for that, Darlin'. Ever since my Earl died from siphoning gasoline, I haven't been able to set foot near that goddamn funeral parlor."

I swallowed hard. Her late ex-husband Earl had siphoned gasoline since he was ten. His family owned the local gas station and apparently, as legend had it, he enjoyed the taste. But on the fateful day in question, he'd been smoking a cigar while he did it...and blew himself to kingdom come. It was U-G-L-Y. Earl was spread all over town. Literally. He and Hattie had been divorced for years and hated each other. It was no secret he had fornicated with over half the older women in town, but when he died like that, he became a saint in her eyes.

I bit down on the inside of my cheek. Hard. Although it was beyond inappropriate, whenever anyone talked about Earl, I laughed.

"Astrid totally understands." Gemma gave Hattie a quick hug and pushed me away from the counter before I said or did something unforgivable.

"Thanks," I whispered. "That would have been bad."

"Yep," Gemma grinned and shoveled a huge spoon of ice cream in her mouth.

"Where in the hell do you put that?" I marveled at her appetite. "You're tiny."

"You're a fine one to talk, Miss I Have the World's Fastest Metabolism."

"That's the only good thing I inherited from the witch who spawned me," I said and dug in to my drug of choice. I winced in pain as my frozen ice cream ass-extender went straight to the middle of my forehead.

"Are you okay?" Gemma asked.

I took a deep breath and pinched the bridge of my nose. God, I hated brain freezes. "No, not right now, but I've decided to change some stuff. Nana would want me to."

My best friend watched me silently over her ice cream.

"I'm going to stop smoking, get a real career, work out every day, date someone who has a job and not a parole officer, get married, have two point five kids and prove that I was adopted."

"That's a pretty tall order. How are you gonna make all that happen?" she asked, handing me a napkin. "Wipe your mouth."

"Thanks," I muttered. "I have no fucking idea, but I will succeed...or die trying."

"Good luck with that."

"Um, thanks. Do you mind if we leave here so I can chain smoke 'til I throw up so it will be easier to quit?"

"Is that the method you're going to use?" Gemma asked, scooping up our unfinished ice cream and tossing it.

"I know it seems a little unorthodox, but I read it worked for Jennifer Aniston."

"Really?"

"No, but it sounded good," I said, dragging her out of Hattie's.

"God, Astrid," Gemma groaned. "Whatever you need to do I'm here for you, but you have to quit. I don't want you to die. Ever."

"Everybody dies," I said quietly, reminded that the woman I loved most had died only a week ago. "But I've got too fucking much to do to die any time soon."

Chapter 1

Three months later...

"There are ten thousand ways to express yourself creatively," I huffed, yanking on my running shoes. "My God, there's acting, painting, sewing, belly dancing, cooking...Shit, scrapbooking is creative." I shoved my arms into my high school sweatshirt that had seen better days.

"You're not actually wearing that," Gemma said, helping herself to my doughnut.

"Yep, I actually am." I grabbed my breakfast out of her hand and shoved it in my mouth. "And by the way, I've decided to be a movie star."

"But you can't act," my best friend reminded me.

"That's completely beside the point," I explained, taking the sweatshirt off. I hated it when Gemma was right. "Half the people in Hollywood can't act."

"Don't you think it might be wise to choose a career that you actually have the skills to do?"

"Nope, I told you I'm making changes. Big ones."

I bent over and tied my running shoes. Maybe if I just ran forever, I would stop hurting. Maybe if I found something meaningful, I could figure out who in the hell I was.

Gemma picked up my soda and took a huge swig. "You're an artist and a damn good one. You should do something with that."

"Yeah, maybe," I said, admiring my reflection in the microwave. Holy hell, my hair was sticking up all over my head. "Why didn't you tell me my hair exploded?"

"Because it's funny," Gemma laughed.

"I'll never make it in show business if people see my hair like this," I muttered and tried to smooth it down.

"Astrid, you will never make it in show business no matter what your hair looks like. You may be pretty, but you can't act your way out of a hole and you suck as a liar," Gemma informed me as she flopped down on my couch and grabbed the remote.

"Your confidence in me is overwhelming." I picked out a baseball cap and shoved it over my out of control curls. "If the movie star thing doesn't work out, I might open a restaurant."

"Did you become mentally challenged during the night at some point?" she asked as she channel surfed faster than any guy I ever dated.

"Gimme that thing." I yanked the remote away from her. "What in the hell are you trying to find?"

"*Jersey Shore.*"

"For real?" I laughed.

"For real for real," she grinned.

"Don't you have a home?" I asked.

"Yep. I just like yours better."

I threw the remote back at her and grabbed my purse. If I was going to be a famous actress, or at the very least a chef, I needed to get started. But before I could focus on my new career, I had business to take care of. Very important business...

"Where are you going?" Gemma yawned. "It's 8:00 on a Sunday morning."

"I'm going running," I said, staring at the ceiling.

"Oh my God," Gemma grinned, calling me out on my lie. "Astrid, since when do you run with your purse?"

"Okay fine," I snapped. "I'm going to run a few errands and say goodbye forever to one of my best friends today."

Gemma gaped at me. Her mouth hung open like she'd had an overdose of Novocain at the dentist. "So today is the day? You really going to end it?"

"I don't really have a choice, since there's so much damn money riding on it."

"Oh my God," she squealed and punched me in the arm. "I'm so proud of you."

"Don't be proud yet," I muttered, praying I'd be successful with my breakup plans.

"You didn't have to take the bet," Gemma said.

"Yes, I did," I said and shook my head with disgust. "Nothing else has worked. Voodoo has to."

"Voodoo?"

"Yep."

"Good luck with that."

"Thanks," I said as I slapped on some lip gloss. "I'm gonna need it."

"Yes, you are," Gemma grinned. "Yes, you are."

***

It was hot and I was sweaty and I wondered for the umpteenth time if I was losing my mind. I needed to stop making bets that were impossible to win. Maybe I could be a social smoker or I could just hide it from everyone. I could carry perfume and gum and lotion and drive to the next town when I needed a nicotine fix.

"Excuse me, are you here to be hypnotized?" a feminine voice purred.

I glanced up from my spot on the filthy sidewalk and there stood the most beautiful woman I'd ever seen. I quickly stubbed out my cigarette, turned my head away in embarrassment and blew my smoke out. Reason number three hundred and forty-six to quit...impersonating a low class loser.

She looked foreign—Slavic or Russian. Huge violet-blue eyes, full lips, high cheekbones set in a perfect heart-shaped face, framed by tons of honey-gold blonde hair. Absolutely ridiculous. I felt a little inadequate. Not only was the face perfect, but the body was to die for. Long legs, pert boobies, ass-o-rific back side and about six feet tall. I was tall at 5 feet 9 inches, but she was *tall*.

"Well, I was," I explained, straightening up and trying to look less like a crumpled homeless mess from my seat on the sidewalk, "but they must have moved." I pointed to a rusted-out doorway.

"Oh no," the gorgeous Amazon giggled. Seriously, did she just giggle? "That's not the door. It's right over here." She grabbed my hand, her grip was firm and cool, and guided me to the correct door. A zap of electricity shot up my arm when she touched me. I tried to nonchalantly disengage my hand from hers, but she held mine fast. "Here we go." She escorted me into the lobby of a very attractive office.

"I don't know how I missed this," I muttered as she briskly led me to a very nice exam room. She released my hand. Did that zap really just happen? Maybe I was already in nicotine withdrawal.

"Please have a seat." The blue eyed bombshell indicated a very soft and cozy looking pale green recliner.

"I'm sorry, are you the hypnotist?" I asked as I sat. Something didn't feel quite right. What was a gorgeous, Amazon Russian-looking chick doing in Mossy Creek, Kentucky? This was a tiny town, surely I would have seen her before.

"Yes, yes I am," she replied, sitting on a stool next to my comfy chair with an official-looking clipboard in her hand. "So you're here because...?"

"Because...um, I want to stop smoking," I told her and then quickly added, "Oh, and I don't want to gain any weight." If you don't ask for the impossible, there's no way you'll ever get it.

Miss Universe very slowly and somewhat clinically looked me over from head to toe. "Your weight looks perfect. You are a very beautiful young woman. Are you happy with your body right now?"

"Yes," I replied slowly. Was she hitting on me? I didn't think so, but...

"That's good," she smiled. "I can guarantee that you will never gain weight again after you're hypnotized."

"Really?" I gasped. My God, that was incredible. Smoke free and at a weight I liked. This was the best day ever.

"Really," she laughed. "Now let's get started."

"Wait, don't I need to fill out a bunch of forms and pay and sign my life away in case you accidentally kill me or something?"

Blondie laughed so hard I thought she might choke. "No, no," she assured me and quickly pulled herself together. "My receptionist is at lunch...we'll take care of it afterwards. Besides, I've never killed anyone by accident."

"Oookay." She was a little weird, but I supposed people with her occupation would be. She did guarantee me I would be smoke free and skinny. That did not suck. Wait...I needed to think this through. I was feeling unsettled and wary. She was odd, made me uncomfortable and had electric hands. On the flip side, she was very pretty, had a really nice office and promised no weight gain. Damn.

Would common sense or vanity prevail? And the winner is...vanity. By a landslide.

She leaned into me, her green eyes intense. I could have sworn her eyes were purple-y bluish. I was getting so tired. I prayed I wouldn't drool when I was out.

"Astrid, you need to clear your mind and look into my eyes," Miss Russia whispered.

"How do you know my name?" I mumbled. "I didn't tell you my name." Alarm bells went off in my brain. My pea-brain that never should have thought it was a good idea to get hypnotized at a strip mall on the bad side of town. You'd think a business called 'House of Hypnotism' might have tipped me off. Crap. These were not the decisions a smart and responsible, if not somewhat directionless, twenty-nine year old woman should make. I should have listened to my gut and gone with common sense.

The room started spinning. It felt like a carnival from hell. Blondie's mouth was so strange. There was something very unattractive going on with her mouth. It got kind of blurry, but it looked like...wait...maybe she was British. They all have bad teeth.

"I fink ooo shud stooop," I said, mangling the English language. I tried again. "Oow do ooo know my name?" When did I put marbles in my mouth? Who in the hell dimmed the lights and cranked the air conditioner?

"Oh Astrid, not only do I know your name," she smiled, her green eyes blazing, "I know everything about you, dear."

Chapter 2

I opened my eyes and immediately shut them. What in the hell time was it? What in the hell day was it? I snuggled deeper into my warm and cozy comforter and tried to go back to sleep. Why couldn't I go back to sleep? Something was wrong...very wrong. I just had no idea what it was.

Ignoring the panic that was bubbling to the surface, I leaned over the side of my bed and grabbed my purse. It was Prada. I loved Prada. I proudly considered myself a Prada whore, *albeit one who couldn't afford it.*

Everything seemed to be in there...wallet, phone, makeup, gum, under-used day planner. Nothing important was missing. I was being paranoid. Everything was fine.

I eyed my beloved out of season Prada sandals lying on my bedroom floor. Shoes always made me feel better. Only in New York or Los Angeles would anyone know my adored footwear was four seasons ago. Certainly not in Istillwearmyhairinamullet, Kentucky. I got them on sale. I paid six hundred dollars that I didn't have for them, but that was a deal considering they were worth a solid twelve hundred.

I pressed my fingers to the bridge of my nose and tried to figure out what day of the week it was. Good God, I had no clue. I suppose exhaustion had finally caught up with me, but I couldn't for the life of me remember what I had done to be so tired. I vaguely remembered driving home from somewhere. I glanced again at my awesome shoes, but even my beautiful sandals couldn't erase the sense of dread in the pit of my stomach.

"Focus on something positive," I muttered as I wracked my brain and snuggled deeper into my covers.

Shoes. Think about shoes...not the irrational suffocating fear that was making me itch. Bargains! That was it, I'd think about bargains. I loved getting a good bargain almost as much as I loved Prada. Unfortunately, I also had a huge love for cigarettes, and I needed to love one now. Right now. I rummaged through my purse and searched for a pack. Bingo! I found my own personal brand of heroin and lit up.

WTF? It wouldn't light because I couldn't inhale. Why couldn't I inhale? Was I sick? I felt my head; definitely no fever. My forehead felt like ice.

Okay, if at first you don't succeed...blah blah blah. I tried again. I couldn't inhale. Not only could I not inhale, I also couldn't exhale. Which would lead me to surmise I wasn't breathing. The panic I was avoiding had arrived.

"Fuck shit fuck fuck, this is a side effect. That's right, a side effect. A side effect of what?" I demanded to no one in particular since I was alone in my room. I knew it was something. It was on the tip of my brain...side effect...side effect of not smoking. Side effect of not smoking? What the hell does that even mean? For God's sake, why can't I figure this out? I have an I.Q. of 150, not that I put it to very good use.

"Wait," I hissed. "It's a side effect of the hypnotism."

God, that was bizarre, but that had to be it. I made that stupid bet with Gemma and got hypnotized to stop smoking by that big blonde Amazon at the House of Hypnotism. That's what I drove home from. I wasn't crazy. The Amazon must have forgotten to inform me that I wouldn't be able to breathe for awhile afterwards. That's what you get when you don't read the fine print. Did I even pay her? I'm sure I'll start breathing any second now. I'm so glad I figured this out. I feel better. For a minute there I thought I was dead.

I glanced out of my bedroom window at the full moon.

"Full moon? Oh my God, have I been in bed all day?"

I threw the covers off and stood quickly, still trying to figure out what day it was. The room spun violently and a wave of dizziness knocked me right back down on my ass. Little snippets of my dreams raced through my mind as I waited for the vertigo to pass.

God, that was a freaky dream. Oprah and Vampyres and yummy, creamy chocolate blood... you couldn't make that stuff up.

The room quit spinning and I stood up slowly, firmly grasping one of the posts of my beautiful four poster bed. I reached up high above my head, arched back and popped my sternum. Slightly gross, but it felt great. I ran my hands through my hair, rubbed the sleep out of my eyes and bit through my bottom lip. Mmm...crunchberries. I licked the tasty blood from my mouth.

I wondered what time it was. If it wasn't too late, I could get a run in and then I could...*bite through my bottom lip?? Crunchberries? What the fu...?*

In my frazzled mental state, I heard a noise in the hallway outside my bedroom. I immediately dropped to a defensive squat on the floor. Way back in high school they told us, if you hear an intruder, get low...or was that for a fire? Shit, that was get low for a fire...what in the hell do I do for a burglar?

Good God, I was in my bra and panties. The blue granny panties with the unfortunate hole in the crotch. Not a good look for fending off burglars. Not a good look ever. On my never ending list of things to do I needed to add *throw out all panties over seven years old.*

I remained low, just in case. I duck walked over to my closet and grabbed one of my many old cheerleading trophies out of a cardboard box so I could kill my intruder. It was plastic, but it was pointy. I'd been meaning to give them to my eight year old neighbor. Thank God I was a procrastinator. Wait a minute...As I death-gripped my trophy I was overwhelmed with the scent of rain and orchids and Pop Tarts and cotton candy.

What the hell?

It wasn't a dream. She was here? And apparently from the smell of it, she had a guest. I'd just cannibalized my own lip, my blood tasted like crunchberries, I could smell people in my house, I couldn't breathe, my skin felt icy, and I think I might be...

"Astrid, are you awake?" Gemma called from right outside my door interrupting my ridiculous train of thought.

Oh thank you, Jesus. "Yes." Was that my voice? It sounded deeper and raspier. And sexier?

"Get out here," Gemma yelled. "Get dressed and change that underwear...it's nasty."

"Gemma, I have to tell you something weird, but you have to believe me and you can't get mad," I said through my closed door, ignoring the insultingly accurate underwear comment.

"I think I already know," she said from the other side.

"It's not about my haircut."

"You got your hair cut without me?" Gemma was appalled.

Shit, I thought she knew about my hair. What did she know then? *Good God, what in the hell was wrong with my bra? The girls were spilling out of it. Were they bigger? Did my bra shrink?* "Gem, um...I swear I meant to tell you about my hair. It was spur of the moment. Mr. Bruce dragged me into the salon and the next thing I knew, he set my baseball cap on fire, cut my hair into long layers and put in some kick ass highlights."

"Fine, Astrid." Her voice got tinny and high. "Just don't be surprised if I go get a perm without you."

"You wouldn't."

"I might," she threatened.

"Gem," I begged, "with me or without me, Do. Not. Get. A. Perm. That's so 1980s."

"You're right," Gemma sighed, "I'd get a lobotomy before I'd get a perm. What do you need to tell me?"

I gathered myself. I realized I was about to sound like an idiot, but when had that ever stopped me? I closed my eyes and let her rip. "Um...after my haircut, I got hypnotized by a big blonde Amazon gal to stop smoking, and now I can't breathe. I think it must be a side effect, but it's freaking me out." Gemma was silent on the other side of my bedroom door.

"You can't breathe?"

"No." I couldn't tell if she believed me.

"Are you sure?"

"I think I would know if I couldn't breathe," I shouted.

"Do I owe you a thousand bucks?"

"I'm not sure yet."

At least I was honest. The entire reason I'd gotten hypnotized was because I'd bet Gemma a thousand dollars I could quit smoking. I knew she thought it was a no-brainer bet due to the sorry fact that this was my ninth attempt to quit in the last three months. Nicotine gum, cold turkey, weaning off and all those self-help books weren't doing it for me. I needed outside assistance. Short of having my lips sewn shut, I hadn't been successful at quitting. Hypnotism was a last resort because having my lips sewn shut was simply not an option.

"Where did you get hypnotized?" she quizzed.

"House of Hypnotism over by the Chinese restaurant that serves cat."

Gemma was speechless. I was getting more nervous with each passing second. "Do you have a pulse?" she asked.

"I'm sorry, what did you just ask me?"

"I said," Gemma yelled through the door, "do you have a pulse?"

"What kind of a stupid question is that? Of course I have a..." I checked for my pulse, then I checked again, then I checked again and then I checked one more time. "Um...no," I whispered.

"You sure?"

"Positive."

"What's your skin temp?"

"Really cold," I told her.

What in the hell was wrong with her? She was awfully calm about the whole thing. She was silent for what felt like an eternity. These questions were right up Gemma's alley. She loved all things weird, especially anything astrological or supernatural. I could tell she was thinking because she was humming 'Billie Jean'. Gemma, besides being a Prada whore who like me couldn't afford it, knew the lyrics to every Michael Jackson song ever recorded. She wore black for an entire year after he died. "I think I know what's going on." She began to hum 'Thriller'.

"What's wrong with me?" I shrieked.

"Come out here, Astrid."

"Wait Gemma...am I dead?"

"Kinda," she said with excitement. The same kind of excitement she exuded when she tried to convince me of Bigfoot's existence. "Just get dressed and get out here."

I quickly whipped on some overpriced jeans that made my butt look asstastic and put on the first shirt my fingers touched. I pulled on some hot pink sequined Converse and made my way out to my living room. That took about ten and a half steps because my house was the size of a postage stamp.

Gemma was standing by the window bouncing like a ball, so excited she was about to burst...and the Queen of Daytime Talk was sprawled on my couch reading my diary. Wait...what?

"Holy Jesus," I gasped. "You're Opr..."

"Don't say it," my idol cut me off, throwing my diary aside as if I wouldn't notice she'd been reading my most private and embarrassing thoughts. "I'm not her, never fuckin' have been, never fuckin' will be. If you call me that, I'll leave. Trust me, that would be very fuckin' bad for you."

"Oookay, you have quite a vocabulary." I smiled, wondering if Gemma thought this was as screwy as I did. She did seem a little freaked, but not nearly enough to merit the fact Oprah was here. "If you're not Opr...I mean that woman who you look exactly like, then you are...?"

I peeked around my tiny living room and looked for cameras. This had to be for a show segment. Right? Gemma must be in on the whole thing with Oprah.

Was she going to redecorate my crappy house or give me a car or tell me something wonderful about my birth mother?

That was impossible. My birth mother was actually the woman who, for lack of a better word, raised me and there wasn't much wonderful about her. My Nana, may she rest in peace, was wonderful. Her daughter, my mother...not so much. Hopefully, Oprah was here to redecorate.

"You're a Vampyre and I'm your fuckin' Guardian Angel," I'm-Not-Oprah grunted.

Gemma squealed and clapped her hands like a two year old at Christmas. Apparently they'd become great friends already, possibly bonding over Bigfoot. The dizziness now combined with total paranoia overtook me as my knees buckled and I dropped to the ground like a sack of potatoes.

"Wow...so not what I was expecting to hear." My stomach was queasy. This was starting to make me tingle, and not in a good way. I'm-Not-Oprah had to go. "Well, golly gee, look at the time; I suppose you have a train to catch...to Crazytown," I informed her in a bizarre cheerleader voice that I had no control over. "So you'd better get going." *Vampyre my ass. I'm-Not-Oprah is cuckoo loco crazy.* I crawled over to my front door and opened it with shaking hands and body, letting Oprah know she had to leave.

I'm-Not Oprah had the gall to laugh, and I don't mean just a little giggle. I mean a huge gut-busting, knee-slapping guffaw. *God, I need a cigarette.* Oh but wait...*I DON'T SMOKE ANYMORE BECAUSE I CAN'T BREATHE.* I was completely screwed. There had to be a logical answer to this clusterfuck. I just needed to think it through.

Ignoring the unexplainable situation in my home, I curled into a ball by my front door and went back through what I could remember. First, I'd gotten my hair cut and colored because it looked like hell. Then I chain-smoked half a pack of cigarettes getting my nerve up to get hypnotized to quit. After almost vomiting from the sheer amount of nicotine in my system, I got hypnotized to stop smoking. Good thinking on my part. Next, the ridiculously attractive Amazon woman who hypnotized me was successful because I will never smoke again. Good thinking on her part.

However, it was also beginning to look like I would never breathe again. So technically I was dead. The lack of pulse and air intake could attest to this, but clearly I wasn't dead because I was curled up on the floor thinking somewhat coherently and Oprah was in my house...What in the hell was I talking about? None of this was possible. I was dreaming. That had to be it. I was dreaming. I pinched myself. Hard.

"Ouch...shit." Not dreaming.

I slowly stood up, determined to kick Her Oprahness out of my house. My whole body began to tremble as I locked eyes with the insane talk show host sitting on my couch. I couldn't believe I was standing here looking at Oprah, who says she's not, who's telling me I'm a Vampyre, which don't exist, and she's a Guardian Angel, which again...don't exist. Besides, if they did, they certainly wouldn't have a mouth like hers.

"Oh my God," I moaned as another bizarre wave of dizziness came over me. The room grew darker and smaller. I'm-Not-Oprah and Gemma started to get blurry and a burning began in my gut. Flames ripped through my stomach and violently shot into my arms, my legs, my neck and head. My insides were shredding. I was thirsty...so very thirsty. God, it hurt so much. I floated above myself as my body crumpled to the floor. The buzzing in my head was deafening. I tried to take a deep breath, but that went nowhere fast.

"I'm dying," I groaned.

Crapballs, did I have good underwear on? No! I still had on light blue grannies with a not on purpose hole in the crotch. Oh my God, I'm dying with bad underpants on. My mother will have a fit. I can hear her now, "*Well, with underpants like that, it's no wonder Astrid couldn't get a man. She kept buying all that Prada, but she should have invested in a couple of pairs of decent panties.*" This was not good.

The blazing inferno inside me consumed my whole body. It was excruciating. I wasn't sure how much more I could take. I vaguely saw Oprah coming for me.

"Kill me please," I begged. She laughed and scooped me up like a rag doll and shoved my face to her neck. God, she smelled good. "Argrah," I gurgled.

"Just shut the fuck up and drink," I'm-Not-Oprah growled.

It was delicious, like rich dark chocolate, so smooth, so warm, so yummy. What was this? The pain slowly subsided and I realized I was curled up in I'm-Not-Oprah's lap with my teeth embedded in her neck. She was rocking me like a baby.

I removed what I'm fairly sure were my fangs from Oprah's neck. "What am I doing?" I calmly asked.

She looked down at me and smiled. Holy cow she looked like Oprah. "Drinking."

"Drinking what?" I inquired politely.

"O negative," she replied.

"O negative what?" I screeched, jerking to an upright position on her very ample lap.

"O negative Angel blood, dumbass," she bellowed. She stood up and dumped me on the floor as she walked over to retrieve my diary.

"Oh my God, you're not joking." I was horrified.

"No, I certifuckingly am not."

Chapter 3

Gemma and I'm-Not-Oprah sat on either side of me on the floor. Gemma held my hand and Oprah just stared.

"Soooo, Gemma, I suppose you've met Opr...I mean, well you know, I mean..." I was dying here. "What I'm trying to say is, you've met...dear God, help me out."

"Pam," they said in unison.

"Pam? Your name is Pam?"

"What's wrong with Pam?" Oprah, *aka Pam*, asked, her eyes narrowing dangerously.

"Nothing," I shot back quickly. That eyeball thing did not look good. "It's just I never expected an Angel to be named Pam."

"What the hell kind of name were you expecting? Tinkerbell?"

"Well, no," I replied. "She's a Fairy. Maybe something like Luna or Sky."

"Holy shit, would you like to be named something like that?" Pam yelled.

I shook my head. God, she was loud.

"You know what I like about you?" she continued.

"No." I feared her answer the same way I feared the IRS, credit card bills and Bryant Gumbel.

"I like that you have the word 'ass' in your name. It opens up so many possibilities."

"That's fantastic. Why are you here again?" I snapped

"I am here," Pam spoke very slowly, as if I were mentally challenged, "to guide your sorry blood suckin', Prada wearin' ass, through the ups and downs of the Vampyre world."

"Well, Mary Sunshine, there's no such thing as Vampyres and..." I started.

"Pam," she interrupted.

"Oookay, *Pam*. I will repeat my earlier sentiment. I'm not a Vampyre, so tell me whatever it is you think you need to tell me and you can go back to Pretend Angel Land."

"Ooooh noooo, Asshead. It don't work like that. I'm here to stay." Pam slapped her knee and hooted like a redneck watching a smack down on WWE.

"Astrid, it's actually really cool," Gemma, my very not dead human friend, tried to convince me over Pam's ruckus. "Pam's been telling me there's this whole Vamp hierarchy thing; Dominions, Havens and...and..."

"Congregants," Pam supplied, calming herself down.

"Right, Congregants and Houses." Gemma kept going. "There's a King, and Warrior Princes, and Princesses."

"Back. Up." I practically spit. "There's a Vampyre King?" I laughed, not believing a word.

"I would suggest you get that out of your system right now, Assface," my Guardian Angel said. "Cause pretty soon a bunch of Vamps are gonna come 'round, and laughing at your King is punishable by death."

"You're joking," I said with a huge grin on my face. I looked at Pam. I looked at Gemma. Pam. Gemma. Pam. Gemma. Nobody was smiling...except me. "You're not joking."

I was no longer smiling. Were they serious or certifiable? Maybe I was crazy. It was difficult to deny that I just drank blood from Oprah's, *I mean*, Pam's neck. And I liked it. Maybe Bigfoot did exist.

Gemma grabbed my hands and forced my focus to her, "Astrid, it's not that bad. A slew of Vampyre girls are going to start arriving soon with gift baskets and invites to parties so you can join their Houses!"

The word gift basket calmed my impending breakdown. "What do you mean, like sorority rush for dead people?" I put my finger in my mouth and felt around for my fangs. I considered this for a moment. Gemma knew I loved free stuff. I was kind of a free sample whore. It was clear from the smug look on her face that she thought she had me at *gift basket*. She couldn't have been more wrong.

"I don't want to be a Vampyre," I yelled, realizing that maybe they weren't yanking my chain. "I want to chain-smoke an entire pack of Marlboro Lights and throw up! I do not want to join some Kappa Alpha Dead House and become BFFs with bloodsucking freaks that smell like the old lady bathroom at the country club." I was on a roll. "That's right...skanky, Gothy Draculas with blood breath, weird bun heads and super long fingernails that curl over at the edges because they should have been trimmed three years ago. And there's no such thing as Vampyres!"

You could have cut the silence with a knife. Gemma looked dazed and Pam...well, Pam just looked confused. Gemma finally roused herself from the visual stupor that my tirade induced. "Dude, that was gross."

"I'm not really following the country club part," Pam stated.

"Don't try," Gemma told her. "I'm getting a Diet Coke, you want anything?"

"Mountain Dew or Budweiser," Pam said.

"I'm on it." Gemma left the room.

"What about me?" I whined. "Don't I get to have anything?"

"You already got to have Pam," Gemma tossed back from my kitchen, laughing like she made a good one.

I sat down on the couch and pouted. What had I done to deserve this? Of course nobody but me would do something to get healthy and end up kind of dead.

"Oh for shit's sake, you're not going to look like some skanky, Goth wannabe bloodsucker. What did the Vamp who changed you look like?" Pam projected as if she were speaking to a crowd of three hundred without a microphone.

159

The sheer volume of her question rendered me speechless for a moment.

"She looked like a Russian supermodel. Wait!" I shouted at Pam. "Do I look different to you?"

"How the hell should I know? I just met you, dumbass," she replied.

"Right. Gemma?" I yelled.

"Behind you," Gemma said, startling me. She handed Pam her beer. *Angels drink beer?*

"Gem, do I look different to you?" I asked.

"Well, you were being such a baby that I wasn't going to tell you, but...You. Are. So. Hot," she screeched. "If I didn't like dangly parts so much, I'd consider switching teams!"

I ran to my bathroom. Holy crap, I was fast. I looked in the mirror and I saw...nothing. Wait a minute...where in the hell was I? Gemma slipped into the bathroom behind me. She showed up in the mirror, but I was M.I.A.

"Dude," Gemma gasped, "you have no reflection."

We stood in silence absorbing this news. I tried several different angles in case there was a trick to it, but no go. It was strange...my clothes were invisible, too. Anything I touched ceased to have a reflection.

"Okay, fine," Gemma said, rubbing my back, "maybe this is the price you have to pay for being so drop dead gorgeous. Oh hell, I didn't mean the dead part...I just meant..."

"It's okay," I said morosely. "Apparently, I am dead." My eyes filled with tears. I pressed my fingers to the bridge of my nose, trying to ward off the panic attack that was hurtling towards earth at frightening speeds. I was headed for a massive freakout.

Gemma grabbed me. "Let me describe you," she said soothingly.

"Okay," I blubbered, wiping my tears. "Oh my God, my eyes are bleeding!" I shouted.

"Shut the hell up," Pam yelled from down the hall. "All Vamps cry blood, cum blood, drink blood. Blood, blood, blood...it's all about blood with you dead people."

"That's disgusting," I said. I looked at Gemma, my eyes wide, "I wonder if I have any other bodily functions?"

"What do you mean?"

"You know, like do I still need to buy toilet paper and tampons?" I answered.

"NOPE," Pam yelled from way down the hall.

"Wow, she's got really good hearing," Gemma grinned. "Do you want to know what you look like?"

"Um...yes."

She stared at me for about a minute and tilted her head to the side. It was a very long minute. She was making me nervous.

"You're beautiful," she said simply. "I mean, you were beautiful before, but it got kicked up a bunch of notches. You're the kind of gorgeous where it's hard to stop looking at you. Your skin," she touched my face, "is paler, but it's perfect. It glows...it's ethereal. Your hair is a darker, richer brown and really shiny. Your lips," she examined my face, "have that I've-just-been-majorly-kissed swollen look. You still have that beauty mark high on your left cheekbone. Your eyes are that really cool amber gold color, but they sparkle now. And if I'm not mistaken, your eyelashes are longer, like they weren't long enough already."

I knew I was being vain, but I glanced toward the mirror again wondering if I just had to warm up or something...Nothing. Shit.

She circled me. "I gotta say, your body's jammin'. Rock hard abs. Legs are still long. Your boobs are definitely bigger and your butt's higher. Overall you're beyond hot." She smiled and squeezed my hands. "What do you feel like?"

Well, that explained my girls trying to escape from my bra. "I feel really strong and fast," I said. "I can hear really well and I can smell things."

"Do I smell?" Gemma did a quick pit check.

"You smell good, like rain and orchids."

"Ooooh, cool." She was delighted. "What does Pam smell like?"

"Pop Tarts and cotton candy. Gem," I paused, "do I have an aura anymore?" One of Gemma's hobbies was reading auras. She could read people before they opened their mouths. She had a gift for it.

"No."

"Is that okay?" I whispered.

"I think so." She hugged me. She felt warm and comfortable.

"Does Pam have one?" I asked.

"Yeah," Gemma answered reverently, "it's a pearly white with shots of purple and pink in it. It's the most beautiful aura I've ever seen. It's truly angelic."

"Do you mean to tell me that foul mouthed Oprah doppelganger really is my Guardian Angel?"

"Yep," Gemma giggled.

"Somebody up there must really hate me," I moaned.

"Yep."

Visit www.robynpeterman.com for more info.

Excerpt from READY TO WERE
Book 1 in the Shift Happens Series

Get your shift in gear and check this series out!

Chapter 1

"You're joking."

"No, actually I'm not," my boss said and slapped the folder into my hands. "You leave tomorrow morning and I don't want to see your hairy ass till this is solved."

I looked wildly around her office for something to lob at her head. It occurred to me that might not be the best of ideas, but desperate times led to stupid measures. She could not do this to me. I'd worked too hard and I wasn't going back. Ever.

"First of all, my ass is not hairy except on a full moon and you're smoking crack if you think I'm going back to Georgia."

Angela crossed her arms over her ample chest and narrowed her eyes at me. "Am I your boss?" she asked.

"Is this a trick question?"

She huffed out an exasperated sigh and ran her hands through her spiked 'do making her look like she'd been electrocuted. "Essie, I am cognizant of how you feel about Hung Island, Georgia, but there's a disaster of major proportions on the horizon and I have no choice."

"Where are you sending Clark and Jones?" I demanded.

"New York and Miami."

"Oh my god," I shrieked. "Who did I screw over in a former life that those douches get to go to cool cities and I have to go home to an island called Hung?"

"Those douches *do* have hairy asses and not just on a full moon. You're the only female agent I have that looks like a model so you're going to Georgia. Period."

"Fine. I'll quit. I'll open a bakery."

Angela smiled and an icky feeling skittered down my spine. "Excellent, I'll let you tell the Council that all the money they invested in your training is going to be flushed down the toilet because you want to bake cookies."

The Council consisted of supernaturals from all sorts of species. The branch that currently had me by the metaphorical balls was WTF—Werewolf Treaty Federation. They were the worst as far as stringent rules and consequences went. The Vampyres were loosey goosey, the Witches were nuts and the freakin' Fairies were downright pushovers, but not the Weres. Nope, if you enlisted you were in for life. It had sounded so good when the insanely sexy recruiting officer had come to our local Care For Your Inner Were meeting.

Training with the best of the best. Great salary with benefits. Apartment and company car. But the kicker for me was that it was fifteen hours away from the hell I grew up in. No longer was I Essie from Hung Island, Georgia—*and who in their right mind would name an island Hung*—I was Agent Essie McGee of the Chicago WTF. The irony of the initials was a source of pain to most Werewolves, but went right over the Council's heads due to the simple fact that they were older than dirt and oblivious to pop culture.

Yes, I'd been disciplined occasionally for mouthing off to superiors and using the company credit card for shoes, but other than that I was a damn good agent. I'd graduated at the top of my class and was the go-to girl for messy and dangerous assignments that no one in their right mind would take... I'd singlehandedly brought down three rogue Weres who were selling secrets to the Dragons—another supernatural species. The Dragons shunned the Council, had their own little club and a psychotic desire to rule the world. Several times they'd come close due to the fact that they were loaded and Weres from the New Jersey

Pack were easily bribed. Not to mention the fire-breathing thing…

I was an independent woman living in the Windy City. I had a gym membership, season tickets to the Cubs and a gay Vampyre best friend named Dwayne. What more did a girl need?

Well, possibly sex, but the *bastard* had ruined me for other men…

Hank "The Tank" Wilson was the main reason I'd rather chew my own paw off than go back to Hung Island, Georgia. Six foot three of obnoxious, egotistical, perfect-assed, alpha male Werewolf. As the alpha of my local Pack he had decided it was high time I got mated…to him. I, on the other hand, had plans—big ones and they didn't include being barefoot and pregnant at the beck and call of a player.

So I did what any sane, rational woman would do. I left in the middle of the night with a suitcase, a flyer from the hot recruiter and enough money for a one-way bus ticket to freedom. Of course, nothing ever turns out as planned… The apartment was the size of a shoe box, the car was used and smelled like French fries and the benefits didn't kick in till I turned one hundred and twenty five. We Werewolves had long lives.

"Angela, you really can't do this to me." Should I get down on my knees? I was so desperate I wasn't above begging.

"Why? What happened there, Essie? Were you in some kind of trouble I should know about?" Her eyes narrowed, but she wasn't yelling.

I think she liked me…kind of. The way a mother would like an annoying spastic two year old who belonged to someone else.

"No, not exactly," I hedged. "It's just that…"

"Weres are disappearing and presumed dead. Considering no one knows of our existence besides other supernaturals, we have a problem. Furthermore, it seems like humans might be involved."

My stomach lurched and I grabbed Angela's office chair for balance. "Locals are missing?" I choked out. My grandma Bobby Sue was still there, but I'd heard from her last night. She'd harangued me about getting my belly button pierced. Why I'd put that on Instagram was beyond me. I was gonna hear about that one for the next eighty years or so.

"Not just missing—more than likely dead. Check the folder," Angela said and poured me a shot of whiskey.

With trembling hands I opened the folder. This had to be a joke. I felt ill. I'd gone to high school with Frankie Mac and Jenny Packer. Jenny was as cute as a button and was the cashier at the Piggly Wiggly. Frankie Mac had been the head cheerleader and cheated on every test since the fourth grade. Oh my god, Debbie Swink? Debbie Swink had been voted most likely to succeed and could do a double backwards flip off the high dive. She'd busted her head open countless times before she'd perfected it. Her mom was sure she'd go to the Olympics.

"I know these girls," I whispered.

"Knew. You knew them. They all were taking classes at the modeling agency."

"What modeling agency? There's no modeling agency on Hung Island." I sifted through the rest of the folder with a knot the size of a cantaloupe in my stomach. More names and faces I recognized. Sandy Moongie? *Wait a minute.*

"Um, not to speak ill of the dead, but Sandy Moongie was the size of a barn…she was modeling?"

"Worked the reception desk." Angela shook her head and dropped down on the couch.

"This doesn't seem that complicated. It's fairly black and white. Whoever is running the modeling agency is the perp."

"The modeling agency is Council sponsored."

I digested that nugget in silence for a moment.

"And the Council is running a modeling agency, why?"

"Word is that we're heading toward revealing ourselves to the humans and they're trying to find the most attractive representatives to do so."

"That's a joke, right?" *What kind of dumb ass plan was that?*

"I wish it was." Angela picked up my drink and downed it. "I'm getting too old for this shit," she muttered as she refilled the shot glass, thought better of it and just swigged from the bottle.

"Is the Council aware that I'm going in?"

"What do you think?"

"I think they're old and stupid and that they send in dispensable agents like me to clean up their shitshows," I grumbled.

"Smart girl."

"Who else knows about this? Clark? Jones?"

"They know," she said wearily. "They're checking out agencies in New York and Miami."

"Isn't it conflict of interest to send me where I know everyone?"

"It is, but you'll be able to infiltrate and get in faster that way. Besides, no one has disappeared from the other agencies yet."

There was one piece I still didn't understand. "How are humans involved?"

She sighed and her head dropped back onto her broad shoulders. "Humans are running the agency."

It took a lot to render me silent, like learning my grandma had been a stripper in her youth, and that all male Werewolves were hung like horses... but this was horrific.

"Who in the hell thought that was a good idea? My god, half the female Weres I know sprout tails when flash bulbs go off. We won't have to come out, they can just run billboards of hot girls with hairy appendages coming out of their asses."

"It's all part of the *Grand Plan*. If the humans see how wonderful and attractive we are, the issue of knowingly living alongside of us will be moot."

Again. Speechless.

"When are Council elections?" It was time to vote some of those turd knockers out.

"Essie." Angela rolled her eyes and took another swig. "There are no elections. They're appointed and serve for life."

"I knew that," I mumbled. Skipping Were History class was coming back to bite me in the butt.

"I'll go." There was no way I couldn't. Even though my knowledge of the hierarchy of my race was fuzzy, my skills were top notch and trouble seemed to find me. In any other job that would suck, but in mine, it was an asset.

"Good. You'll be working with the local Pack alpha. He's also the sheriff there. Name's Hank Wilson. You know him?"

"Yep." *Biblically. I knew the son of a bitch biblically.*

***

"You're gonna bang him."

"I am not gonna bang him."

"You are so gonna bang him."

"Dwayne, if I hear you say that I'm gonna bang him one more time, I will not let you borrow my black Mary Jane pumps. Ever again."

Dwayne made the international "zip the lip and throw away the key" sign while silently mouthing that I was going to bang Hank.

"I think you should bang him if he's a hot as you said." Dwayne made himself comfortable on my couch and turned on the TV.

"When did I ever say he was hot?" I demanded as I took the remote out of his hands. I was not watching any more *Dance Moms*. "I never said he was hot."

"Paaaaleese," Dwayne flicked his pale hand over his shoulder and rolled his eyes.

"What was that?"

"What was what?" he asked, confused.

"That shoulder thing you just did."

"Oh, I was flicking my hair over my shoulder in a *girlfriend* move."

"Okay, don't do that. It doesn't work. You're as bald as a cue ball."

"But it's the new move," he whined.

Oh my god, Vampyres were such high maintenance. "According to who?" I yanked my suitcase out from under my bed and started throwing stuff in.

"Kim Kardashian."

I refused to dignify that with so much as a look.

"Fine," he huffed. "But if you say one word about my skinny jeans I am so out of here."

I considered it, but I knew he was serious. As crazy as he drove me, I adored him. He was my only real friend in Chicago and I had no intention of losing him.

"I know he's hot," Dwayne said. "Look at you—you're so gorge it's redonkulous. You're all legs and boobs and hair and lips—you're far too beautiful to be hung up on a goober."

"Are you calling me shallow?" I snapped as I ransacked my tiny apartment for clean clothes. Damn it, tomorrow was laundry day. I was going to have to pack dirty clothes.

"So he's ugly and puny and wears bikini panties?"

"No! He's hotter than Satan's underpants and he wears boxer briefs," I shouted. "You happy?"

"He's actually a nice guy."

"You've met Hank?" I was so confused I was this close to making fun of his skinny jeans just so he would leave.

"Satan. He's not as bad as everyone thinks."

How was it that everyone I came in contact with today stole my ability to speak? Thankfully, I was interrupted by a knock at my door.

"You expecting someone?" Dwayne asked as he pilfered the remote back and found *Dance Moms*.

"No."

I peeked through the peephole. Nobody came to my place except Dwayne and the occasional pizza delivery guy or Chinese food take out guy or Indian food take out guy. *Wait. What the hell was my boss doing here?*

"Angela?"

"You going to let me in?"

"Depends."

"Open the damn door."

I did.

Angela tromped into my shoebox and made herself at home. Her hair was truly spectacular. It looked like she might have even pulled out a clump on the left side. "You want to tell me why the sheriff and alpha of Hung Island, Georgia says he won't work with you?"

"Um...no?"

"He said he had a hard time believing someone as flaky and irresponsible as you had become an agent for the Council and he wants someone else." Angela narrowed her eyes at me and took the remote form Dwayne. "Spill it, Essie."

I figured the best way to handle this was to lie— hugely. However, gay Vampyre boyfriends had a way of interrupting and screwing up all your plans.

"Well, you see..."

"He's her mate and he dipped his stick in several other...actually *many* other oil tanks. So she dumped his furry player ass, snuck away in the middle of the night and hadn't really planned on ever going back there again." Dwayne sucked in a huge breath, which was ridiculous because Vampyres didn't breathe.

It took everything I had not to scream and go all Wolfy. "Dwayne, clearly you want me to go medieval on your lily white ass because I can't imagine why you would utter such bullshit to my boss."

"Doesn't sound like bullshit to me," Angela said as she channel surfed and landed happily on an old episode of *Cagney and Lacey*. "We might have a problem here."

"Are you replacing me?" Hank Wilson had screwed me over once when I was his. He was not going to do it again when I wasn't.

"Your call," she said. Dwayne, who was an outstanding shoplifter, covertly took back the remote and flipped over to the Food Channel. Angela glanced up at the tube and gave Dwayne the evil eye.

"I refuse to watch lesbians fight crime in the eighties. I'll get hives," he explained, tilted his head to the right and gave Angela a smile. He was so pretty it was silly—

piercing blue eyes and body to die for. Even my boss had a hard time resisting his charm.

"Fine," she grumbled.

"Excuse me," I yelled. "This conversation is about me, not testosterone ridden women cops with bad hair, hives or food. It's my life we're talking about here—me, me, me!" My voice had risen to decibels meant to attract stray animals within a ten-mile radius, evidenced by the wincing and ear covering.

"Essie, are you done?" Dwayne asked fearfully.

"Possibly. What did you tell him?" I asked Angela.

"I told him the Council has the last word in all matters. Always. And if he had a problem with it, he could take it up with the elders next month when they stay awake long enough to listen to the petitions of their people."

"Oh my god, that's awesome," I squealed. "What did he say?"

"That if we send you down, he'll give you bus money so you can hightail your sorry cowardly butt right back out of town."

Was she grinning at me, and was that little shit Dwayne jotting the conversation down in the notes section on his phone?

"Let me tell you something," I ground out between clenched teeth as I confiscated Dwayne's phone and pocketed it. "I am going to Hung Island, Georgia tomorrow and I will kick his ass. I will find the killer first and then I will castrate the alpha of the Georgia Pack...with a dull butter knife."

Angela laughed and Dwayne jackknifed over on the couch in a visceral reaction to my plan. I stomped into my bathroom and slammed the door to make my point, then pressed my ear to the rickety wood to hear them talk behind my back.

"I'll bet you five hundred dollars she's gonna bang him," Dwayne told Angela.

"I'll bet you a thousand that you're right," she shot back.

"You're on."

Chapter 2

"This music is going to make me yack." Dwayne moaned and put his hands over his ears.

Trying to ignore him wasn't working. I promised myself I wouldn't put him out of the car until we were at least a hundred miles outside of Chicago. I figured anything less than that wouldn't be the kind of walk home that would teach him a lesson.

"First of all, Vampyres can't yack and I don't recall asking you to come with me," I replied and cranked up The Clash.

"You have got to be kidding." He huffed and flipped the station to Top Forty. "You need me."

"Really?"

"Oh my god," Dwayne shrieked. "I luurrve Lady Gaga."

"That's why I need you?"

"Wait. What?"

"I need you because you love The Gaga?"

Dwayne rolled his eyes. "Everyone loves The Gaga. You need me because you need to show your hometown and Hank the Hooker that you have a new man in your life."

"You're a Vampyre."

"Yes, and?"

"Well, um...you're gay."

"What does that have to do with anything? I am hotter than asphalt in August and I have a huge package."

While his points were accurate, there was no mistaking his sexual preference. The skinny jeans, starched muscle shirt, canvas Mary Janes and the gold hoop earrings were an undead giveaway.

"You know, I think you should just be my best friend. I want to show them I don't need a man to make it in this world...okay?" I glanced over and he was crying. Shitshitshit. Why did I always say the wrong thing? "Dwayne, I'm sorry. You can totally be my..."

"You really consider me your best friend?" he blubbered. "I have never had a best friend in all my three hundred years. I've tried, but I just..." He broke down and let her rip.

"Yes, you're my best friend, you idiot. Stop crying. Now." Snark I could deal with. Tears? Not so much.

"Oh my god, I just feel so happy," he gushed. "And I want you to know if you change your mind about the boyfriend thing just wink at me four times and I'll stick my tongue down your throat."

"Thanks, I'll keep that in mind."

"Anything for my best friend. Ohhh Essie, are there any gay bars in Hung?"

This was going to be a wonderful trip.

***

One way in to Hung Island, Georgia. One way out. The bridge was long and the ocean was beautiful. Sun glistened off the water and sparkled like diamonds. Dwayne was quiet for the first time in fifteen hours. As we pulled into town, my gut clenched and I started to sweat. This was stupid—so very stupid. The nostalgic pull of this place was huge and I felt sucked back in immediately.

"Holy Hell," Dwayne whispered. "It's beautiful here. How did you leave this place?"

He was right. It was beautiful. It had the small town feel mixed up with the ocean and land full of wild grasses and rolling hills. How did I leave?

"I left because I hate it here," I lied. "We'll do the job, castrate the alpha with a butter knife and get out. You got it?"

"Whatever you say, best friend. Whatever you say." He grinned.

"I'm gonna drop you off at my Grandma Bobby Sue's. She doesn't exactly know we're coming so you have to be on your best behavior."

"Will you be?"

"Will I be what?" God, Vamps were tiresome.

"On your best behavior."

"Absolutely not. We're here."

I stopped my crappy car in front of a charming old Craftsman. Flowers covered every inch of the yard. It was a literal explosion of riotous color and I loved it. Granny hated grass—found the color offensive. It was the home I grew up in. Granny BS, as everyone loved to call her, had raised me after my parents died in a horrific car accident when I was four. I barely remembered my parents, but Granny had told me beautiful bedtime stories about them my entire childhood.

"OMG, this place is so cute I could scream." Dwayne squealed and jumped out of the car into the blazing sunlight. All the stories about Vamps burning to ash or sparkling like diamonds in the sun were a myth. The only thing that could kill Weres and Vamps were silver bullets, decapitation, fire and a silver stake in the heart.

Grabbing Dwayne by the neck of his muscle shirt, I stopped him before he went tearing into the house. "Granny is old school. She thinks Vamps are...you know."

"Blood sucking leeches who should be eliminated?" Dwayne grinned from ear to ear. He loved a challenge. Crap.

"I wouldn't go that far, but she's old and set in her geezer ways. So if you have to, steer clear."

"I'll have her eating kibble out of my manicured lily white hand in no time at...holy shit!" Dwayne screamed and ducked as a blur of Granny BS came flying out of the house and tackled my ass in a bed of posies.

"Mother Humper." I grunted and struggled as I tried to shove all ninety-five pounds of pissed off Grandma Werewolf away from me.

"Gimme that stomach," she hissed as she yanked up my shirt. Thank the Lord I was wearing a bra. Dwayne stood in mute shock and just watched me get my butt handed to me by my tiny granny, who even at eighty was the spitting image of a miniature Sophia Loren in her younger years.

"Get off of me, you crazy old bag," I ground out and tried to nail her with a solid left. She ducked and backslapped my head.

"I said no tattoos and no piercings till you're fifty," she yelled. "Where is it?"

"Oh my GOD," I screeched as I trapped her head with my legs in a scissors hold. "You need meds."

"Tried 'em. They didn't work," she grumbled as she escaped from my hold. She grabbed me from behind as I tried to make a run for my car and ripped out my belly button ring.

"Ahhhhhhgrhupcraaap, that hurt, you nasty old bat from Hell." I screamed and looked down at the bloody hole that used to be really cute and sparkly. "That was a one carat diamond, you ancient witch."

Both of her eyebrows shot up and I swear to god they touched her hairline.

"Okay, fine," I muttered. "It was cubic zirconia, but it was NOT cheap."

"Hookers have belly rings," she snapped.

"No, hookers have pimps. Normal people have belly rings, or at least they used to," I shot back as I examined the wound that was already closing up.

"Come give your granny a hug," she said and put her arms out.

I approached warily just in case she needed to dole out more punishment for my piercing transgression. She folded me into her arms and hugged me hard. That was the thing about my granny. What you saw was what you got. Everyone always knew where they stood with her. She was mad and then she was done. Period.

"Lawdy, I have missed you, child," she cooed.

"Missed you too, you old cow." I grinned and hugged her back. I caught Dwayne out of the corner of my eye. He was even paler than normal if that was possible and he had placed his hands over his pierced ears.

"Granny, I brought my…"

"Gay Vampyre best friend," she finished my introduction. She marched over to him, slapped her hands on her skinny hips and stared. She was easily a foot shorter than Dwayne, but he trembled like a baby. "Do you knit?" she asked him.

"Um…no, but I've always wanted to learn," he choked out.

She looked him up and down for a loooong minute, grunted and nodded her head. "We'll get along just fine then. Get your asses inside before the neighbors call the cops."

"Why would they call the cops?" Dwayne asked, still terrified.

"Well boy, I live amongst humans and I just walloped my granddaughter on the front lawn. Most people don't think that's exactly normal."

"Point," he agreed and hightailed it to the house.

"Besides," she cackled. "Wouldn't want the sheriff coming over to arrest you now, would we?"

I rolled my eyes and flipped her the bird behind her back.

"Saw that, girlie," she said.

Holy Hell, she still had eyes in the back of her head. If I was smart, I'd grab Dwayne, get in my car and head back to Chicago…but I had a killer to catch and a whole lot to prove here. Smart wasn't on my agenda today.

Chapter 3

The house was exactly the same as it was the last time I saw it a year ago. Granny had more crap on her tables, walls and shelves than an antique store. Dwayne was positively speechless and that was good. Granny took her décor seriously.

"I'm a little disappointed that you want to be a model, Essie," Granny sighed. "You have brains and a mean right hook. Never thought you'd try to coast by with your looks."

I gave Dwayne the *I'll kill you if you tell her I'm an agent on a mission* look and thankfully he understood. While I hated that my granny thought I was shallow and jobless, it was far safer that she didn't know why I was really here.

"Well, you know...I just need to make a few bucks, then get back to my life in the big city," I mumbled. I was a sucky liar around my granny and she knew it.

"Hmmm," she said, staring daggers at me.

"What?" I asked, not exactly making eye contact.

"Nothin'. I'm just lookin'," she challenged.

"And what are you looking at?" I blew out an exasperated sigh and met her eyes. A challenge was a challenge and I *was* a Werewolf...

"A bald face little fibber girl," she crowed. "Spill it or I'll whoop your butt again."

Dwayne quickly backed himself into a corner and slid his phone out of his pocket. That shit was going to video my ass kicking. I had several choices here...destroy Dwayne's phone, elaborate on my lie or come clean. The only good option was the phone.

"Fine," I snapped and sucked in a huge breath. The truth will set you free or result in a trip to the ER... "I'm an agent with the Council—a trained killer for WTF and I'm good at it. The fact that I'm a magnet for trouble has finally paid off. I'm down here to find out who in the hell is killing Werewolves before it blows up in our faces. I plan to find the perps and destroy them with my own hands or a gun, whichever will be most painful. Then I'm going to castrate Hank with a dull butter knife. I plan on a short vacation when I'm done before going back to Chicago."

For the first time in my twenty-eight years on Earth, Granny was mute. It was all kinds of awesome.

"Can I come on the vacation?" Dwayne asked.

"Yes. Cat got your tongue, old woman?" I asked.

"Well, I'll be damned," she said almost inaudibly. "I suppose this shouldn't surprise me. You are a female alpha bitch."

"No," I corrected her. "I'm a lone wolf who wants nothing to do with Pack politics. Ever."

Granny sat her skinny bottom down on her plastic slipcovered floral couch and shook her head. "Ever is a long time, little girl. Well, I suppose I should tell you something now," she said gravely and worried her bottom lip.

"Oh my god, are you sick?" I gasped. Introspective thought was way out of my granny's normal behavior pattern. My stomach roiled. She was all I had left in the world and as much as I wanted to skin her alive, I loved her even more.

"Weres don't get sick. It's about your mamma and daddy. Sit down. And Dwayne, hand over your phone. If I find out you have loose lips, I'll remove them," she told my bestie.

I sat. Dwayne handed. I had thought I knew everything there was to know about my parents, but clearly I was mistaken. Hugely mistaken.

"You remember when I told you your mamma and daddy died in a car accident?"

"Yes," I replied slowly. "You showed me the newspaper articles."

"That's right." She nodded. "They did die in a car, but it wasn't no accident."

Movement was necessary or I thought I might throw up. I paced the room and tried to untangle my thoughts. It wasn't like I'd even known my parents, but they were mine and now I felt cheated somehow. I wanted to crawl out of my skin. My heart pounded so loudly in my chest I was sure the neighbors could hear it. My parents were murdered and this was the first time I was hearing about it?

"Again. Say that again." Surely I'd misunderstood. I'd always been one to jump to conclusions my entire life, but the look on Granny's face told me that this wasn't one of those times.

"They didn't own a hardware store. Well, actually I think they did, but it was just a cover."

"For what?" I asked, fairly sure I knew where this was going.

"They were WTF agents, child, and they were taken out," she said and wrapped her skinny little arms around herself. "Broke my heart—still does."

"And you never told me this? Why?" I demanded and got right up in her face.

"I don't rightly know," she said quietly. "I wanted you to grow up happy and not feel the need for revenge."

She stroked my cheek the way she did when I was a child and I leaned into her hand for comfort. I was angry, but she did what she thought was right. Needless to say, she wasn't right, but...

"Wait, why would I have felt the need for revenge?" I asked. Something was missing.

"The Council was never able to find out who did it, and after a while they gave up."

Everything about that statement was so wrong I didn't know how to react. They gave up? What the hell was that?

The Council never gave up. I was trained to get to the bottom of everything. Always.

"That's the most absurd thing I've ever heard. The Council always gets their answers."

Granny shrugged her thin shoulders and rearranged the knickknacks on her coffee table. Wait. Did the Council know more about me than I did? Did my boss Angela know more of my history than I'd ever known?

"I knew that recruiter they sent down here," Granny muttered. "I told him to stay away from you. Told him the Council already took my daughter and son-in-law and they couldn't have you."

"He didn't pay me any more attention than he did anyone else," I told her.

"What did the flyer say that he gave you?"

"Same as everybody's—salary, training, benefits, car, apartment."

"Damn it to hell," she shouted. "No one else's flyer said that. I confiscated them all after the bastard left. I couldn't get to yours cause you were shacking up with the sheriff."

"You lived with Hank the Hooker?" Dwayne gasped. "I thought you just dated a little."

"Hell to the no," Granny corrected Dwayne. "She was engaged. Left the alpha of the Georgia Pack high and dry."

"Enough," I snapped. "Ancient history. I'm more concerned about what kind of cow patty I've stepped in with the Council. The *sheriff* knows why I left. Maybe the Council accepted me cause I can shoot stuff and I have no fear and they have to hire a certain quota of women and…"

"And they want to make sure you don't dig into the past," Dwayne added unhelpfully.

"You're a smart bloodsucker," Granny chimed in.

"Thank you."

"You think the Council had something to do with it," I said. This screwed with my chi almost as much as the Hank situation from a year ago. I had finally done something on my own and it might turn out I hadn't earned any of it.

"I'm not sayin' nothing like that," Granny admonished harshly. "And neither should you. You could get killed."

She was partially correct, but I was the one they sent to kill people who broke Council laws. However, speaking against the Council wasn't breaking the law. The living room had grown too small for my need to move and I prowled the rest of the house with Granny and Dwayne on my heels. I stopped short and gaped at my empty bedroom.

"Where in the hell is my furniture?"

"You moved all your stuff to Hank's and he won't give it back," Granny informed me.

An intense thrill shot through my body, but I tamped it down immediately. I was done with him and he was surely done with me. No one humiliated an alpha and got a second chance. Besides, I didn't want one... Dwayne's snicker earned him a glare that made him hide behind Granny in fear.

"Did you even try to get my stuff back?" I demanded.

"Of course I did," she huffed. "That was your mamma's set from when she was a child. I expected you'd use it for your own daughter someday."

My mamma...My beautiful mamma who'd been murdered along with my daddy. The possibility that the Council had been involved was gnawing at my insides in a bad way.

"I have to compartmentalize this for a minute or at least a couple of weeks," I said as I stood in the middle of my empty bedroom. "I have to do what I was sent here for. But when I'm done, I'll get answers and vengeance."

"Does that mean no vacation?" Dwayne asked.

I stared at Dwayne like he'd grown three heads. He was getting terribly good at rendering me mute.

"That was a good question, Dwayne." Granny patted him on the head like a dog and he preened. "Essie, your mamma and daddy would want you to have a vacation before you get killed finding out what happened to them."

"Can we go to Jamaica?" Dwayne asked.

"Ohhh, I've never been to Jamaica," Granny volunteered.

They were both batshit crazy, but Jamaica did sound kind of nice...

"Fine, but you're paying," I told Dwayne. He was richer than Midas. He'd made outstanding investments in his three hundred years.

"Yayayayayayay!" he squealed.

"I'll call the travel agent," Granny said. "How long do you need to get the bad guy?"

"A week. Give me a week."

Excerpt from HOW HARD CAN IT BE?

Book 1 of Handcuffs and Happily Ever Afters

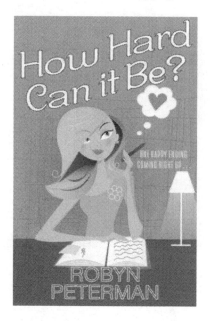

Edition Notice

Chapter 1

"If you handcuff a woman to the headboard, you need to use fur-covered cuffs. Otherwise you'll rub all the skin off of her wrists during rough sex and she'll bleed like a mother fucker. Blood is just not sexy unless you're writing paranormal." The gal with the lesbian hair cut laid that little nugget out with gusto.

What in the hell am I doing here? I'm going to kill Oprah. Does anybody actually listen to her 'if you can visualize it you can do it' crap other than me? Becoming a famous romance novel writer sounded like such a good idea the other day. The simple fact that I couldn't really write seemed beside the point...

My best friend and roommate, Kristy, accused me of pulling a Sunshine Weather Girl again. That was a low blow. I didn't like to think about that. Clearly showing up at the news station for a month straight wasn't the way to become the new weather girl. It did result in a restraining order, six hours in the pokey and a feature story on the Six O'clock news. My mother told all her friends I was adopted...I wasn't.

So here I stood, in the poorly lit back meeting room of the downtown public library, with ten or so women who look like seventy year old church ladies. Why do women in the mid-west think that really short hair shaved up at the back of the neck is a good look? I found out the bondage gal's name was Sue, but she went by Shoshanna

LeHump. Quite the little fire ball, she was dressed entirely in lavender fleece. She explained her husband had threatened to divorce her if she continued to write that garbage under her real name. Her words, not mine. I didn't know if I was more shocked by her pen name or the fact that she was married.

I glanced around the room hoping to spot Evangeline O'Hara, the famous New York Times bestselling author. She wrote a mean bodice ripper and was the main reason I'd joined this group. I hoped she'd like my ideas and mentor me to stardom. Of course ideas were a slight problem at this point, but I would continue visualizing like hell.

I was looking forward to discussing Evangeline's books with her, until Kristy, not unkindly, reminded me I hadn't read any of them.

"Turkey Noodle Dooda Surprise served with Tatertot Casserole can really get your amorous juices flowing," the one who called herself Nancy gushed. Her floral caftan reminded me of Hawaii. The quintessential grandma had no last name. Apparently she had legally changed her name to Nancy...you know, like Cher or Beyoncé or Gaga.

"I'm sorry," I interrupted. "I thought this was a romance writers meeting." My insides clenched. This couldn't be right. I must be in the wrong room, or hopefully the wrong building.

"It is," Shoshanna LeHump said. "Nancy writes romantic cookbooks!"

"Oh, aren't you a lovely thing." Nancy smiled and squeezed my hands. "Are you a cover model?"

"Um, no. I'm actually a um...writer," I white lied. I do write things. I'm a CPA, for God's sake. I just happened to write numbers instead of words.

"Shoshanna," Nancy called out to the handcuff loving porno granny, "we have a new writer!"

"Fucking awesome," the Shoshanna woman yelled back, giving me a big thumbs up.

Shit, this was not turning out the way it was supposed to. These women were very sweet, they'd all hugged me when I arrived like I was a long lost friend. Okay, that was a little unsettling, but as well meaning as they were, I didn't want a Bunko group of Grandmas who cussed like sailors...I wanted Dorothy Parker Round table, where we drank wine and chuckled at our own witty brilliance. Speaking of witty brilliance, where in the hell was the Queen of Bodice Rippers? I'm not sure how much more information my brain can hold about bondage, whippings and marshmallow jello molds before it explodes.

"Excuse me," I cut in on Shoshanna LeHump's in-depth explanation of the benefits and sanitation of butt-plugs, "I thought Evangeline O'Hara was a member."

The room went silent. Everyone stared at me like I'd grown three heads. All of the lumberjack-looking softball-playing grandmas narrowed their eyes at me.

"Are you friends with that viper bitch whore from hell?" Nancy, the storybook granny, inquired kindly. The words and the tone did not match. Clearly I'd heard her wrong, but on the off chance I hadn't, I refused to ask her to repeat herself.

"Um...no," I whispered, a little bit scared. "I've never met her. I just thought she was a member."

Everyone's smiles returned when they realized I wasn't best buds with the viper bitch whore from hell. These seniors had some amazing vocabularies. I made a mental note not to get on their bad side.

"Oh, thank God," Shoshana LeHump grumbled. "I was worried that stinky hooker sent a spy in to steal more of our ideas."

"What do you mean?" I asked, shocked. What kind of ideas would a New York Times bestselling author steal from old ladies with butt-plugs and cookbooks?

"She's a criminal," Poppy Rose Petal yelled. God, I hope that's her pen name. She was a big boned gal with a blinding fuchsia neck scarf, trim kakis, baby pink sweater and loafers...with a shiny penny in each. "That last book she wrote was Shoshana's idea."

"That's true," Ms. LeHump, the handcuff expert, ground out angrily. "The bus tour across Russia was my baby and she stole it. Of course my bus is a rolling S and M club for amputees, but the basic premise is the same."

It was time for me to get out of here. If Evangeline O'Hara was even one-fourth as bat-shit crazy as the rest of these gals, I needed to make a break for it.

"So," Poppy the Flower woman asked, "Rena, what are you writing?"

"Well...um--" What in the hell was I going to say? I didn't want to give away any of my brilliant ideas. Wait...I didn't actually have any ideas. Time for a butt-yank explanation. Not to be confused with butt-plug. "It's a romantic comedy about a school teacher and um...a bus driver." In my nervousness I spoke a little louder than I'd intended. Evidenced by several of the old girls discreetly covering their ears. Shit.

"Sounds great," Nancy exclaimed. My God, could she be nicer? "What's the plot?"

"The plot." What was the plot? That was an excellent question. "Well, it's a forbidden love...because he's a former convict and um, they vow to have sex in every room in the school."

"Fantastic," Shoshana LeHump yelled, slapping her thighs and doing what looked like a drunken Irish jig. "Are there any threesomes or girl on girl action?"

"No." I bit the inside of my cheek to keep from laughing. "That hadn't occurred to me."

"Well--" she winked at me-- "a little girl on girl action can really spice up a story."

Was she hitting on me? I couldn't tell. It seemed like she was, but she's married. I'm fairly sure she used the word husband at one point between her diatribes on cock rings and lubricants. To avoid that train of thought I continued on with my big fat hairy lie of a plot.

"Anyway, it turns out he was unjustly accused of a mass murder during a hurricane and spent the last five or ten years in prison. Maybe it was seven years...I can't remember exactly. Then he dug his way to freedom, using a spork, right before his sentence was overturned, but now they want to put him back in prison for breaking out. You see, he didn't know they were going to let him out of the pokey. That's why he tunneled to freedom." I sucked in a deep breath and scanned the room for alternate exits. Maybe I could slip out when they weren't looking...

"Oh my God," the Rosebush Petal woman said, "that's incredible. How does he meet the teacher?"

"Of course," I stammered, "the teacher. So he dyes his hair and gets his teeth capped. He had a gap between his two front teeth because his parents couldn't afford braces when he was a child, and he steals an identity. He goes to the school and gets a job as the bus driver after about four interviews. He's really worried about the background check because he doesn't know all that much about the person he stole the identity from."

"Intrigue, that's good." Nancy nodded her approval.

"Thanks," I said, smiling. Her genuine kindness and encouragement made me feel like an ass for lying, but I was already in too deep. "Then he sees the teacher across the playground during third period and it's love at first sight."

"Does she have big boobs?" Shoshanna LeHump asked.

"Um...yes. Yes, she does." I sucked my bottom lip into my mouth and put on my serious face. She had definitely been hitting on me.

"Wait--" My potential girlfriend stopped me. "I thought you said romantic comedy. Where's the funny part?"

"Oh, the funny part...right." What is the funny part? Shit, shit, shit. "The funny part is when they...um have, you know, sex in all the classrooms. Chalk and erasers get in the way, mayhem ensues. The fire alarm goes off. The chairs are too small...Stuff like that." I was sweating now. I wasn't sure how much more crap I could come up with.

"Does he have to go back to prison?" a rather rotund gal with kind eyes and no eyebrows named Joanne asked. She clearly had a violent relationship with her tweezers. More impressive was her purple Minnesota Vikings sweat suit. It made her look like a giant grape.

"No, no he doesn't," I said with finality, hoping we'd move on to someone else.

"Does the teacher ever find out about his past?" Nancy inquired.

"Nope." I smiled. "I'm going for that ambiguous feeling. Kind of like real life."

"Fucking brilliant," Shoshanna bellowed. "I still think you should consider a little threesome action. Maybe with the principal or one of the lunch ladies."

"You might be right." My enthusiasm sounded forced, but I hoped if I agreed, she would shut up.

"You should listen to LeHump," Poppy the Plant said. "She made three hundred thousand in sales last year alone."

"What?" I gasped. I had no idea so many people wanted to read about sticking things in their butt. As impressed as I was with that number, I couldn't possibly add a scene with the teacher and the bus driver and the lunch lady. It wasn't true to my vision. What am I talking about? I have no vision. I just pulled the most ridiculous premise out of my rear end and now I have a vision?

As I silently contemplated the merits of a threesome with the lunch lady, the mood in the room changed abruptly. The tension grew thick and the hair stood up on my arms. The women scurried around like ants in a rainstorm. What was going on? Were they offended that the bus driver didn't come clean about his past? I could change that part. Maybe he should tell her...After all, he's not really guilty of killing anybody. I mean, he did steal an identity, but he found the driver's license in the garbage in back of a Wendy's restaurant when he was scrounging for food. He was starving, for God's sake...couldn't they understand that?

"She's here," Nancy hissed. All eyes flew to the door.

"Who's here?" I whispered urgently. My breakfast doughnut was threatening to make a reappearance. Why in the hell didn't I leave at the first mention of bondage? I was scared to death and I had no idea why.

"The skanky, book stealing, bottom feeding slag," Shoshanna LeHump said quietly. "Don't look her in the eye-- she'll suck out your soul."

"Put Rena behind you," Nancy frantically barked to Shoshanna. Her muumuu flowed wildly around her, making me dizzy. "The smelly skank-hole always goes for the new ones. Protect her!" she hissed.

LeHump shoved me behind her. She was strong for such a tiny thing. I was starting to hyperventilate. What in the hell had I gotten myself into?

A small almost inaudible whimper rippled through the room as she entered...Ladies and Gentlemen...Evangeline O'Hara is in the house.

Chapter 2

An eerie hush fell over the room. I could feel Poppy the Azalea Bush trembling next to me and Joanne was picking at her face where her eyebrows used to be. Nancy and LeHump held their ground, but they were half the women they had been only five minutes ago. We stood huddled together like a herd of cows. There was a lump in my throat and my heart was bouncing around in my chest like a ping pong ball; I knew everyone could hear it. What in the hell was happening? With extreme caution I peeked out from behind Shoshanna's head.

What the fuck was that? That couldn't possibly be Evangeline O'Hara. Could it? My God, the picture she uses on her website has to be at least thirty years old...maybe forty.

She prowled the room like a panther...with a limp. It had to be the shoes. I'd only seen shoes like that in magazines. They were so high, I didn't know how she didn't teeter off. Her body was skeletal thin. But her boobs...her boobs were ginormous and didn't move as she circled the mound of terrified women pressed together in the middle of the room. She was draped in turquoise silk. The same color as her eyes. I'm positive she slept with them open, not by choice...by necessity. They'd been lifted to her eyebrows. She looked like she'd just come out of a supersonic wind tunnel; her face was yanked back as tight as a drum. There wasn't a line on her forehead or around her eyes or mouth, but her neck resembled a flesh colored rotten prune. Clearly her vision was impaired, because if she got a gander at her neck...Hoo Betty. My guess was that misplaced pride in her frighteningly abundant cleavage blinded her to the saggy neck.

There's just something inherently wrong with an eightyish year old woman sporting the triple D bosom of a twenty year old centerfold model. Although to be fair, she was kind of cadaver-ish chic, similar to Cher.

Her mouth was a train wreck. It was a cross between a fish and a duck and it didn't quite close. Between the mouth and the eyes, she appeared to be in a constant state of surprise. Her plastic surgeon should be shot. I idly wondered if food fell out when she ate, although it didn't look like she ate much. I couldn't look away. I pulled on my bangs, forcing my eyes to the floor, trying desperately not to make eye contact. There was no doubt she could suck out a soul.

"Hello dahalllings," she purred, and her voice was a mix of Harvey Firestein and Marilyn Monroe. Her bodyguard, a big burly man in a black suit somewhere in his fifties, quickly put his arm out to steady her as she almost took a tumble off her designer stilettos. "Shoshinka, my love, how are we doing today?"

"Fine," Shoshanna growled, "until about three minutes ago. And my name is Shoshanna."

"Of course," Evangeline laughed. It reminded me of ice breaking off of trees after a horrific winter storm. Deadly. "You have such an amusing sense of humor, Shoshushu."

Shoshanna's body tensed like a coil about to spring. I gently put my hand on her back to calm her. Her small body shook beneath my touch. Why were these women so scared and why were they taking this mean old biddy's crap? I held my breath, watching in fascination as Evangeline's bulging eyes scanned the crowd. Nancy pushed me down so the scary hag wouldn't see me. Their protectiveness confused and touched me. Their fear was palpable, but my own terror began to ebb away...replaced by anger.

Five minutes ago this room was filled with joyful, kind women who had passions for butt-plugs and dishes made with Cream of Mushroom soup. They'd taken me in and hadn't laughed at my book idea, and it certainly wasn't much of an idea. Although with some work... Focus, I needed to focus. I needed to save these women. These gals were protecting me. They didn't even know me and they'd thrown their bodies in front of mine so the viper bitch whore from hell (Nancy's words, not mine) couldn't eat me.

My sense of justice had gotten me in trouble before, but that was baby stuff compared to what was about to go down...

"So girls--" Evangeline seated herself with a lot of help from her bodyguard. I knew my eyes should be trained on the floor like the rest of the group, but I couldn't keep myself from looking. I wish I had. Her silk sheath hiked up during her descent to the chair, exposing an ungodly amount of spray tanned, pickled thigh. She crossed her toothpick legs and I realized with sickening clarity, she was going commando. I bit my lip to tamp down my gag reflex, but I knew it would be weeks before I had an appetite again. "I'm curious if anyone has any new ideas."

She waited.

And waited.

"I bet you are," Shoshanna muttered under her breath.

"What was that, Shorunka darling?" she asked, grinning evilly. "I thought I heard something unpleasant."

"It must have been your conscience, dear." Nancy smiled, speaking in a loving tone.

"I don't think she has one," Rosebush Flower Petal burst out, her voice sounding fragile and shaky.

"I don't think she has one," Evangeline mimicked Rose Flower Gal with an evil hiss. "Well, she doesn't. And all of you stupid, unattractive old women should know that by now, so cough up the ideas," she shrieked.

Eyebrow-less Joanne was hyperventilating behind me and Flower Power seemed seconds away from fainting. This would be funny if it wasn't real, but it was...very real, and these lovely, albeit strange, older gals were terrified. If

195

these ladies couldn't stand up for themselves, I'd do it for them...

"I have an idea." I shimmied my way out of the huddle and stood in front of her. Holy shit, up close she looked like a wax figure from Madame Tussaud's Museum.

"No, Rena, no," Shoshanna moaned in agony. An icy blast of fear shot through me at Shoshanna's tone, but I figured if I gave Evangeline my idea, maybe she would leave, and my cute little ladies could have fun again.

"Ah, what have we here?" Evangeline eyed me from head to toe. She enviously fingered my long blonde hair and winced at my snow-boots. "Some new blood. How lovely of you ladies to bring me a gift. Especially one as breathtakingly beautiful as this one."

Good God, are all these old women lesbians?

"She's not for you," Shoshanna said through clenched teeth, stepping forward to stand next to me. "She's not even a writer."

Ouch, that stung. Of course Shoshanna is correct, I'm not a writer. I know she's trying to save me from the plastic surgery experiment gone awry seated in the chair, but I wish she had come up with a less hurtful defense. I put my arm around my little bondage-loving new buddy in solidarity and to let her know I'm fine.

"I'll be the judge of that," the viper spat, pushing Shoshanna away from me with the pointed toe of her shoe. I quickly averted my eyes to avoid the peep show she insisted on performing. "What's your name, pretty girl?" Evangeline asked in a silky voice.

"Rena," I could hardly raise my voice above a whisper. Maybe this wasn't such a good idea.

"Rena what?" she pried. The bodyguard took out a pad and pen from his breast pocket.

"Rena Gunderschlict." There was an audible groan of dismay from the pile of ladies behind me. I knew my last name was awful, but I didn't think their reaction was to my name...it was the fact I'd given it to the idea stealing hag.

I experienced a surge of panic as the bodyguard wrote it down on his pad. He was formal and official, causing me a hellacious flashback to my recent arrest downtown at the news station after my pathetic attempt to become the new Sunshine Weather Girl.

"So Rena, my dear," her strangely hypnotic voice urged me on, "what's your idea?"

There was no way in hell I was going to tell her about the teacher and the convict bus driver. I wasn't not sure if the girls were blowing smoke up my butt about my story or if it's a best seller in the making. Just in case, I wasn't giving it to the walking Botox experiment. I'd simply have to yank another one out of my rear...

"Well...um...there's this pirate," I started.

"Yes?" In her excitement she leaned forward, giving me an unfortunate view of the perky round globes attached to her eighty year old bony chest.

"Yep, a pirate," I said, looking everywhere except at Evangeline's bosom. I rocked back and forth in panic, having no idea what was going to come out of my mouth. "And he kidnaps these beautiful twins during an earthquake. It was about a four or so on the Richter scale. He's never seen anything as gorgeous as these young women in his life." I glanced over at Shoshanna, who discreetly moved her hands to her breasts. "They had ginormous breasts."

"Ahhh, yes." Evangeline cooed. "Tell me more."

"Right, so...he steals them in the middle of the night from their mansion in Sydney Australia. Once he gets them on the ship, he realizes they're conjoined." I stared at the ceiling, praying for divine intervention, or a power outage.

"Holy shit," Shoshanna choked.

"Be quiet, Shoshoodoo," the viper hissed. "Continue," she demanded.

"At this point he realizes he only loves one of them. The other one is a total bitch."

Evangeline clasped her hands greedily. "What's her name?"

"Whose name?" I asked.

197

"The name of the one he loves." She rolled her eyes at my stupidity.

That was really alarming. Bulging eyeballs with permanently open lids should not be permitted to roll. Ever. "Oh, her name is, um...Shirley, but it just so happens that the pirate is a time traveling vampire warlock."

"I've never heard of that." Intense astonishment touched her waxy face.

"Of course you haven't," I stammered. A wave of apprehension swept through me and I started to sweat. "There's only one in existence."

Her head whipped around to her bodyguard, "Are you getting all this, Cecil?" He nodded his huge head and kept writing.

Cecil? His name is Cecil? That so didn't work for me. He looked like a Butch or a Rocky. "So..." I had no idea what was going to come out of my mouth next. I needed to wrap this baby up or I was going to pass out from anxiety. "The pirate--"

"What's his name?" the pantyless meanie asked.

"Um...Dave, his name is Pirate Dave. So Pirate Dave time travelled to the future with the conjoined twins to John Hopkins Hospital."

"What year?" she asked, reaching out to touch me with her claw.

I backed away, feigning deep thought. "1974."

"Why 1974?" She sounded bewildered.

"Pardon my rudeness, but if you keep talking, I will never finish." I made eye contact and held it. She narrowed her eyes. I narrowed mine...and waited.

"Fine," she snapped, "I'll be quiet."

"Good. Anyway Pirate Dave held his massive sword to the surgeon's neck and demanded that he separate the twins. So the surgeon did and Dave gave him three bags of gold and some Elvis trading cards he found when he visited the 1950's. He magicked up some limbs for his love and her bitch of a sister because...um...it would be too hard to live a regular life, you know, missing half a torso and arms and legs and half of your butt and..." I stopped. The entire room watched me, mouths agape. I didn't take that as a good sign...I skipped the rest of their physical description. "So they time travelled back to the year they were from."

"What year?" Evangeline bounced up and down with excitement. Her boobs did not.

I paused and gave her the evil eye. Her bouncing stopped and she looked passably contrite. "Sorry," she muttered.

"The year was 1492. The very same year that Columbus sailed the ocean blue. But what most people don't know is that Pirate Dave discovered America, not Columbus...not Leif Ericson."

The crowd gasped. I can't believe they're buying this shit. I wonder how far I can go... "If you think about it, it makes perfect sense. Pirate Dave is a time traveling vampire warlock. He's already been to America in the future a bunch of times and he knows exactly where it is. He doesn't want to take credit for the discovery because he likes being a pirate too much. He garners great enjoyment out of kidnapping beautiful women and having sex with them. He has a medical problem that causes a constant erection and he has to have sex four to six times a day."

"Is this based on a true story?" Evangeline inquired.

"Yes, yes it is." I nodded, biting the inside of my cheek so hard I drew blood.

"I thought so," she said, impressing herself with her vast knowledge of history.

"So when they got back to the ship, Pirate Dave and Shirley started to have sex on the deck of the ship while everyone watched. They were so in love, they couldn't wait to ravish each other and they were so into each other, they didn't even realize anyone was watching."

"How romantic." Evangeline was breathing hard,;her left hand cupped her right breast.

Ewwww, she was turned on. I was going to shower for a long time tonight.

"Then they lived happily ever after. The end."

"Wait," Evangeline shouted. "What happened to the bitch sister?"

I hesitated. What in the hell happened to the evil sister? Shit. "She...um, tried to kill Pirate Dave and Shirley while they were having intercourse on the deck, but the crew got so mad they threw her overboard. They were all voyeurs."

"Did she die?" a high squeaky voice asked. Who in the fuck said that? Cecil? Cecil sounded like a ten year old nerd before puberty. The voice did not match the body. He and Evangeline were quite the pair.

"That's for me to know and you to find out in the sequel," I said. As if.

"What's the sister's name?" Cecil asked.

What the hell was it with these people and names? "Laverne, her name is Laverne."

Cecil gave me a big shit eating grin. "Laverne and Shirley? You named them Laverne and Shirley?"

If he wasn't connected to the viper bitch whore from hell, he might just be okay...but he was with her, and therefore the enemy. "Yes." I couldn't help but return his grin. I could hear the stifled giggles from behind me. Evangeline looked confused and pissed about being left out of something.

"What are you idiots laughing at?" she snapped. "This is based in truth. I remember reading about all this in high school. Rena has no imagination! She just looked up facts and is trying to make you think she's created a masterpiece." Her voice was shrill.

My God, she was stupid and evil, never a good combination.

"Jeeves--" She unconsciously grabbed both of her breasts and her eyes got glassy. The images she was embedding in my brain would take years of therapy to remove...and I thought his name was Cecil. "We've not done a paranormal yet. They're very popular right now," she hissed with excitement. "This will be my crowning glory! I will be bigger than Jackie Collins!"

Cecil-Jeeves nodded and continued to write. Wait...was it really a good idea? I basically just coughed up a hairball of idiocy and she planned to turn it into a New York Times best seller? You know, maybe it was good. The whole time traveling vampire warlock thing hadn't been done yet. I'd just come up with the next big thing and this over-Juvedermed shrew was going to steal it. I'd never read a romance novel about conjoined twins. It was a huge market that had never been tapped. I just came up with the new Twilight and it was slipping through my fingers. This would make a riveting movie. What in the hell was I thinking, giving my entire future away like that? The whole separation of the twins and the murder plot was truly inspired. There was absolutely nothing like it out there. Thank God I hadn't told her about the teacher and the convict bus driver—that would be a hit for sure. She was going to steal my story and make millions off of it. My millions. Damn it, that was not going to happen.

"There's just one little problem," I replied sharply, cutting into her Jackie Collins fantasy. "It's my idea and I'm writing the book."

Evangeline's nostrils flared with fury and she glared at me. The little ladies gasped and without even seeing them, I knew they had huddled closer together in abject terror. Cecil-Jeeves raised an eyebrow and Shoshanna swallowed a laugh that ended up sounding like the first gag of a throw up.

"You're right, Rhonda--" Evangeline's voice was like honey-- "but you're a nobody. Never been published. Sholulu here says you're not even a writer."

It was funny how she couldn't remember anyone's name, but she could recall every word they said. I had a bad feeling Shoshanna's comment would come back to haunt me.

"When I said that--" Shoshanna leapt to my defense-- "I was simply referring to her unpublished status....at the moment."

"Of course you were, Shoshanka." Evangeline had turned on a dime. She now sounded sane, rational and sweet. WTF? "Reba darling--" She smiled and extended her claws to me. I so did not want to touch her, but politeness dictated my decision. I gingerly took her hands. I'm a good mid-western girl, after all. Her hands were ice cold and I tried to block out the fact that they'd been cupping her bosom only moments ago. "You're right," she continued gently. "It is your idea and it's brilliant. I'd like to offer you something...something rare and special. Something I offer to no one. Would you like that, Rona?"

"I don't know," I answered, half in anticipation, half in dread. The room became so quiet, I thought everyone had left. Nope, they were still here, they'd just stopped breathing. So had I.

"I'd like to mentor you on your book," she purred.

My ladies gasped. I don't know if it was in envy or horror. Although, if I was a gambling girl, I'd put my money on horror. I noticed Cecil's jaw clench. He continued to write, but his body language suggested anger. What was that about? Was he jealous? Ew, did he have a thing going with her and didn't want to share? I needed to stop this line of thought before my gag reflex kicked in.

"I don't know..." I started.

"We will write together," she quickly interjected. "You and I will share co-author credit. I already have an agent, a publishing house, publicity team, website and a fan base of millions. You would be a short sighted fool not to take me up on this...That is, unless you're not really an author," she challenged, watching me carefully.

I was still freaked out that she liked the pirate idea. Was she brain damaged? Even though I loved the idea of being a rich and famous author, I wasn't sure selling my soul to the devil was the best way to go about it. I knew deep down inside that the Pirate Dave-Laverne and Shirley conjoined twins concept sucked. And while I was being brutally honest with myself, the bus driver-teacher thing was pretty horrid too. Shoshanna was right. I'm not a writer. I'm an accountant. I just wish there was a little more excitement in my life...

"Um...thanks for your interest, but no. I already have a job and I am saving my vacation days for a trip to see the Tommy Bartlett Show at the Wisconsin Dells." Oh my God, did I just say the Tommy Bartlett Show? The cheesy water show with the skiing squirrel? Yes, I did...I had just revealed my total inner-dork. Why didn't I lie and say Aruba or someplace sexy?

I began biting my cuticles in panic. I didn't belong here. All these women, eyebrows or not, were authors...real authors, who could actually write. Not young, bored-with-their-life girls who were desperately searching for something to feel passionate about. That being said, I wasn't about to let the skanky witch have my idea. I'd give it to one of the girls here. Shoshanna would love it; there could definitely be some girl on girl action in this one. Although the conjoined twins thing made it a bit complicated. I noticed everyone in the room was breathing again and Cecil's jaw had relaxed. Everyone seemed happy, except the viper bitch whore from hell.

"I'll pay you," she spat. "I'll pay you ten thousand dollars a week for three weeks." The happy relaxed atmosphere in the room disappeared abruptly. My stomach clenched and I felt dizzy. That is a shit load of money. "You'll be at my home every day from eight am till five pm. We will write the book. We will split the profits fifty-fifty and then you will be free to go to the Tommy Bartlett Show," she sneered.

Damn it to hell, why did I say Tommy Bartlett Show? That would be hard to live down...God, I could make more than half a year's salary in three weeks...if I sold the witch my soul. I'd done plenty of stupid things for free, why not do something massively stupid and make a butt-load of money doing it? Could I stand being around her for that long? I was a little curious to see if food dropped from her mouth when she ate...I could probably see her without make up. No, that would be nightmare inducing. Shoshanna took my hand.

"If she goes, I go with her," she said in a steely tone.

"Delightful," Evangeline trilled evilly, "that makes me very happy, Shrilanka. I'll see you both on Monday." She stood with an enormous amount of help from Cecil or Jeeves or whatever his name was and sauntered out of the room.

"Wait," I gasped when I found my voice, but she was gone. "I never said I would do it. Shit, shit, shit." I paced

203

the room in anxiety. "Shoshanna, I can't go work with that thing." My cuticles found their way back to my teeth.

"Relax Rena, I'll be with you. I wouldn't leave you alone with that heinous cow bitch from the underworld. Do you really have vacation time?" LeHump asked and I nodded. I couldn't speak because my mouth was full of fingers. "Good, then you can make a bunch of money and we can get our lives back from that skank." Shoshanna rubbed her hands together with glee. "This could kill two birds with one stone."

"What in the hell are you talking about?" I was still in shock that by not speaking up I might have fucked my life for the next three weeks, although I'd be richer for it.

"The first bird is the money for you," Shoshanna explained excitedly; then she began to fidget. "Rena--" LeHump's fidgeting increased-- "I don't want you to get offended by what I'm about to say..."

"Okay," I said, feeling a little nauseous and bracing myself to be heartily offended.

"We could effectively end her career with that paranormal Pirate Dave-Laverne and Shirley story. It's the worst pile of shit I've ever heard," she exclaimed with intense pleasure. "We help her write it, take absolutely no credit..."

"Like she would have given you any credit anyway," Nancy chimed in.

"True--" Shoshanna was on a roll. "The toothpick with knockers takes full credit, gets it published and goes down in flames!"

"This could solve all of our problems," Petunia Tree Bush yelled, eyes blazing with joy.

"Possibly," Nancy said cautiously, "but it could backfire."

"How could bringing her down with conjoined twins and a time traveling vampire warlock with erectile dysfunction backfire?" Shoshanna was confused. Clearly she thought my story was a no-brainer career killer.

Fine. I knew it wasn't a good idea, but to have it paraded around as the crowning jewel that could bring a career down in flames was humiliating. More so, because I knew it was true. And what was this backfire talk? I felt the heat crawl up my neck and I bit my bottom lip so I wouldn't cry. It didn't work.

"Oh dear heavens," Eyebrow-less Joanne, the purple grape, grabbed me in a bear hug and rocked me back and forth. "LeHump, you made her cry." She held me in a vice-like grip and I was having a hard time breathing. These ladies were strong.

"Oh fuck," LeHump was distraught, "Rena, I'm so sorry. Were you serious about that story? I had no idea. I thought for sure you just made that pile of crap up as you went along." LeHump started to cry. "I feel awful," she sobbed.

They all started to cry. The room was filled with snot nosed, weeping seventy year olds...and it was my fault. The viper whore bitch from Hades had nothing on me. I brought an entire roomful of sweet women to tears and because of Joanne's stranglehold, I couldn't breathe well enough to tell them it was alright.

"Can't breathe," I wheezed, trying to extricate myself from my comforter.

"Jesus Christ on a cross," Poppy Bush shrieked, "you're killing her!"

Joanne screamed, dropped me to the floor and started to wail. Holy hell, this was worse than speed dating for Lutherans. I landed on all fours at her feet. I felt light headed and had to remain in doggie position for a few moments before the dizziness subsided.

"It's okay, guys." I struggled to my feet. "It's okay," I repeated. "I did pull it out of my ass and I knew it sucked...it's just hard to hear somebody else say it out loud." I drew in a huge shaky breath and wondered if Joanne had crushed my lungs. "Plus, I'm a little pre-menstrual." I dropped into the chair that Evangeline had vacated minutes ago as all the ladies nodded in understanding.

"I feel like a douche bag," Shoshanna groaned, her shoulders slumped; she wiped her tears on the sleeve of her lavender fleece pullover.

"You're not a douche bag," I said, the beginnings of a smile pulling at my lips.

"I'm a total douche bag," she muttered, running her hands through her hair and making it stand up on end. "A thoughtless stinky douche bag."

"I'd say you're just a douche, not a douche bag." I giggled at her description of herself and the scary hairdo.

The rest of the girls began to smile and chuckle. Shoshanna grinned at me gratefully and took my hand. "I really am sorry. I have a malady called diarrhea of the mouth. I am insensitive and loud and...I'm sorry. It's not that bad an idea. With some work..."

"Stop," I laughed, smacking her little hand. "I'll be more hurt and insulted if you lie to me. The idea sucks and if you guys want me to feed it to her, I will. God knows I could use the money, but how will we get away with this? She's got to know the idea is awful."

"Are you kidding me?" Joanne couldn't control her burst of laughter. "You think she has taste? She's under the very mistaken assumption that her plastic surgeon is a genius!"

"Joanne's right," Poppy Rose Vine laughed. Her voice was rich and warm, almost masculine. She was anything but, with her trim bod and pink feminine clothes. "She thinks she looks forty!"

"She smokin' crack," I laughed. I twisted my hands and racked my brain, but I couldn't for the life of me remember Poppy's whole name. I don't know why, perhaps it's because it doesn't fit her. "What's your real name, Poppy?" I asked, wondering if it fit her any better.

A blush covered her face and I noticed she could use a really good lip wax. "Um...," she stammered, looking around for support. Had I gotten too personal? "I've changed it several times--" she smiled shyly-- "but lately I've been going by Harriet. It was my mom's name."

"It's lovely," I told her. She was fragile for such a big gal. She was by far the largest of the women. Not fat, just big boned and strong. Harriet was easy to remember. It didn't really fit her either, but it was better than all the floral names I had running around in my head. "May I call you Harriet?"

"Yes, you may," she paused, "but would you mind terribly calling me Poppy Harriet?"

"I think that could be arranged." I smiled. God, I felt like I'd known these women forever. What was that about? "So, back to the matter at hand," I rallied my newfound troops. "If she's going to buy a time traveling vampire warlock with a permanent hard-on who likes to have intercourse with recently separated conjoined twins that he had to magic up some body parts for, what else do you think I can get away with?"

My posse of gals grinned evilly and we started to plan.

Chapter 3

After the meeting Shoshanna walked me to my car, letting me know what to expect Monday morning. Thank God she did. Damn thing was totally dead.

"Son of a bitch," I groaned, banging my head on the steering wheel.

"Don't worry about it, Rena, I'll drive you home," LeHump offered.

I glanced up at Shoshanna. There she stood, bundled up in a lime green down coat with a Minnesota Vikings matching hat, glove and scarf set. Her snow boots were a Pepto Bismol pink. Never had I seen an ensemble so hideous and so lovely at the same time. First impressions aren't often wrong, but they can be. I had definitely been wrong about LeHump. She might write porno and have a bad haircut, but she also had a huge heart and I don't think she was hitting on me. I think she was just weird.

"Where do you live?" I asked.

"New Hope. Where do you live?"

"Saint Paul," I sighed. I was going to be cabbing it, or possibly even worse...bussing it. Shit. New Hope was thirty minutes in the opposite direction from my house and I lived a half hour from where we were. There was no way I could let her drive me home.

"That would add an hour onto your trip. I can't let you do that." I smiled and squeezed her purple and gold clad hand.

"It's no fucking biggie. My sister lives in Saint Paul. she'll be thrilled if I stop by. She owes me money. Plus I need to get you a little more up to speed about the slag."

"Shoshanna, it's really too far."

"Bullshit. Just hang on a second. I need to move my computer and baseball bat out of the front seat."

Shoshanna was not taking no for an answer, which was very sweet...I thought. The baseball bat concerned me, but I figured if she was going to kill me she would have already done it in the parking garage. There was no one in sight and no security cameras anywhere.

I grabbed my tote and my purse and hustled over to Shoshanna's sky blue Mazda minivan. I could have called AAA, but I didn't have enough body fat to sit in sub-zero temperatures for three hours and wait for them. As it was, my snot was freezing as I walked the thirty feet to Shoshanna's soccer-mom-ish mode of transport. I needed to move to a warmer climate.

"Get in. It takes a while for the heat to work in this piece of shit, but when it kicks in, you'll sweat like a fat whore at confession."

"Do you eat with that mouth?" I grinned, shaking my head and searching for the seat belt. The car was a pig sty.

Shoshanna cackled with glee, "You bet I do! Are you going to remember all the new stuff you came up with?"

"It would be very difficult to forget the part about the three-way between Pirate Dave, Leif Ericson and Christopher Columbus," I choked out, still searching for the seat belt.

"That's some good stuff there, Rena. I don't think I could have come up with that one myself. You have the scariest imagination I've ever had the pleasure to witness."

"Um...thanks." A compliment is a compliment no matter how insulting.

"The part that really gets me is when the pirate with scurvy and no fingers on his left hand tries to sew the twins back together. That is just fucking gross."

"Is it too gross?" I worried. Maybe that was going a little too far. I had gotten kind of carried away, but when

Poppy Harriet's Dr. Pepper flew out of her nose, I couldn't stop myself. Maybe I should try stand-up comedy...

"Absolutely not!" Shoshanna bellowed. "I'd go even a little farther. Give him lice or severe halitosis, a club foot maybe."

"LeHump, that's gross."

"You're right--" She grinned sheepishly. "I don't have it like you do."

"I'm not real sure that coming up with plots that can bring careers down in flames is 'having it,' but thank you." I still couldn't find the damn seatbelt, but I did find a few rock hard fries and what may have been a cheeseburger during the 1980's. "LeHump, your car is disgusting."

"I've been meaning to clean it out. What in the hell are you digging for?"

"The seat belt."

"Oh." She shrugged guiltily, "I cut them out. Everybody's doing it."

"Oookay." I didn't have a comeback for that one, so I simply smiled and nodded. She's nuttier than my Aunt Phyllis, who is convinced there are little people in her T.V. I was beginning to wonder about her sanity and my own for getting into her car.

I told her where I lived and she proceeded to drive like a bat out of hell. I prayed the entire time. I no wasn'tt particularly religious, but when my life was in danger I figured it couldn't hurt.

"So, we'll probably do some light housecleaning and possibly bathe her turd-laying, skank-breath rat dogs. Bring your lunch because the viper bitch doesn't keep food in the house. Oh, wear sweats, but bring a nice outfit. She likes to make us run errands. Don't ever say no to an errand."

My mouth was agape and an icy chill ran up my spine. "Are you serious?" What had I gotten myself into?

"As a heart attack." Shoshanna made a gagging sound. I thought she was going to vomit. "Once Joanne refused to drive in a blizzard to get gourmet treats for those shit eating canines and Evangeline made her scrape her bunions for an hour. That's the day Joanne started pulling her eyebrows out."

"I thought maybe that was a fashion choice."

"Oh, God no. She had wonderful bushy eyebrows before the bunion incident."

I wasn't not sure I would put the words wonderful and bushy eyebrows together, but I also wouldn't be caught dead in a lime green coat driving a light blue minivan. Then again, who was I to judge? I've been tapped as the girl with career destroying ideas.

"Okay, sweats, nice clothes, lunch and never say no to an errand. I got it. Will we do any writing?" I put my feet up on the dash, hoping it might break the blow from the accident we were sure to have. She'd already run two red lights and flipped off more drivers than I did in an entire month.

"We'll sit down with Cecil and dictate to him. She sleeps most of the time when she's not having procedures done or yelling at us." LeHump leaned over, turned the heat down and almost swerved into a convenience store.

"Shoshanna," I shrieked. I saw my life flash before my eyes and was thankful I was wearing good underpants. I would hate to die in holey granny panties. My mom would shit a brick.

"Sorry--" She grinned, "I was getting hot. So anyway like I was saying..."

"Wait." I cut her off,. This was not making sense to me. "Why are you guys all doing stuff for her? Does she pay you?"

Shoshanna shifted uncomfortably in her seat. "Not exactly. Let's just say it's a business arrangement."

"Well that's fairly cryptic," I deadpanned.

"I love that word," LeHump gushed. "Don't you love that word?"

"Sure." I raised my not bushy brow sarcastically. "Do you also like the word 'avoidance'?"

"Love it," LeHump laughed. "It's my favorite."

***

"Holy fuck." Shoshanna grabbed my arm and yanked me to a halt as we rounded the corner to walk into my building. "Smokin' hot butt dead ahead."

"Oh my God," I gasped. She was right. It's a little creepy to have someone my grandparent's age ogle the behind of a thirty-ish year old guy, but she was correct. It was the finest ass I'd ever seen.

"He's going into your building," she hissed, hopping up and down with excitement.

Mr. Sexy-ass used a key and went in. That meant he lived there. That amazing ass lives in my building! From the back he was Adonis. Unless he was sporting a unibrow and no teeth, my guess was he was hot from the front too. "You know he's probably gay," I said pulling Shoshanna toward the front door just in case we could get another glimpse. No such luck.

"I don't think so. That ass looked very straight to me," she said. I refrained from asking why she thought that. I was more afraid of her answer than the thought of the butt being gay.

Shoshanna came up to my apartment to use the loo. It was the least I could offer, after she'd gone so far out of her way for me. I was grateful for the ride, but even more grateful to still be alive. In a mere matter of hours Shoshanna had grown on me...kind of like a fungus. A non-deadly, sweet smelling, insane fungus. I liked her and actually looked forward to spending time with her in the next three weeks, despite the scary circumstances. There was no telling what would come out of her mouth. I enjoyed not being the only loose cannon in the room.

"Oh my God!" Kristy gasped. "Professor Sue?"

"Kristy!" LeHump shouted joyously, embracing my roommate in a bear hug, "How are you? I haven't seen you in years. What are you doing now? I still remember that thesis you wrote on women's roles throughout religious history. One of the best goddamned papers I ever read."

Kristy blushed furiously and preened under LeHump's praise. What in the hell was going on here? LeHump was a porno writer, not a professor...Wait a minute. Was LeHump the famous 'Professor Sue' I'd heard about ad nauseam from Kristy's college days? No freakin' way.

"Shoshan...Sue, you know my roommate?" Damn, I'd almost blown her cover. I was very curious as to her real last name, but asking would be bizarre at this point.

"Know her? Know her?" Shoshanna yelled. Dang, she was loud. "Not only do I know her, she was one of the best students I ever had."

Kristy looked positively orgasmic and I was flabbergasted. Had I moved into an alternate universe? The sum so did not equal the parts. I thought today couldn't get any weirder.

I thought wrong.

"Rena," my star-struck roommate gushed, "this is the Professor Sue. One of the most respected and sought after professors of Women's Studies in the country. Her work has been published worldwide."

I glanced at Shoshanna/Sue. The irony was almost too much to bear. She winked and put her finger to her lips. I got it...Clearly Kristy was not referring to the butt plug trilogy or the contortionist sex-slave series LeHump had regaled me with when she wasn't trying to run us off the road during our thirty minute ride from hell.

"I didn't realize you had a day job." I grinned at LeHump, shaking my head and removing my snow boots. She smirked and gave me a thumbs up. She was crazy.

"Where's the john? I'm about to pee in my pants!"

"Down the hall and to the left," I interjected quickly. LeHump had no manners or social graces and while I liked her, I wouldn't put it past her to relieve herself on my kitchen floor. I am so not cleaning that up. I yanked her coat off and shoved her down the hall.

Kristy ran around the kitchen like a chicken with its head cut off, pulling open cabinets and sniffing things she pulled from the fridge.

"Hey, we have a new neighbor with a rockin' hot ass."

"I have no time to discuss body parts. Help me," she hissed frantically, slapping cheese and Wheat Thins on our best platter. "Damn it," she muttered, staring at the green mold on the corner of the hunk of cheddar. I grabbed a knife and cut it off.

"Voila!" I curtsied and tossed the offending cheese in the trash. "My Aunt Phyllis taught me that."

"Isn't she the one with people in her radio?"

"T.V., not radio."

Kristy rolled her eyes, "That certainly makes all the difference." She stopped moving and I watched her brain go into rewind. "What do you mean, you saw the neighbor's ass?"

"We have a new neighbor named Mr. Asstastic." Fully clarifying I hadn't humped the new neighbor.

"Did you introduce yourself to his ass?" she asked, rearranging the hors d'oeuvres on the platter.

"Hell no. I never even saw his face."

"The face is good, I met him earlier, but I didn't get to see his ass. When you see the face, you'll jump him. Hell, when he sees you, he'll probably jump you first." I rolled my eyes and she fussed some more with the tray. "Is this classy enough?"

"Trust me, Sho...Sue will love it. I've been in her car." I went for some Wheat Thins, only to get slapped down by Kristy. "So, she's really a professor?" The paradox was mind boggling.

"Not just a professor, she's one of the foremost authorities on Women's Studies in the United States. There are waiting lists to get into her classes at the U. Oh my God." She froze. "Is Professor Sue in your writing group?"

Hmm, how to answer that without giving up LeHump's passion for all things anal? Thankfully I didn't have to.

"You bet I am!" Shoshanna loudly informed us as she marched directly to the cheese, cut herself a few slices and shoved them in her mouth. "I love cheese." She grabbed a handful of Wheat Thins and made herself comfortable on the couch. I guess she was staying.

"So Kristy, I hope to the great God Almighty you are using your amazing brain to make the world a better place." LeHump put her little feet up on the coffee table. "You guys got anything sweet?"

"Yes, doughnuts. And get your damn feet off the table. Do you live in a barn?" I grabbed a box of powdered sugar minis and tossed them to her.

"Rena!" Kristy screeched at decibels that could result in hearing loss. Her mortification made her eye twitch. Not a good look. "I'm so sorry, Professor Sue, for Rena's horrific, disgusting, appalling behavior. Please, put your feet anywhere you like." She shot me a look of death.

Shoshanna/Sue LeHump chuckled and dug into the doughnuts. "Oh Kristy, Rena's right. I tend to fall on the side of uncouth. I could use a good handler to keep me in line."

I made a face at Kristy and I literally felt her need to slap me. She wouldn't dare, not in front of the legendary Professor Sue What-ever-her-last-name-was.

I decided to make nice with my roomie. Last time I pissed her off, she froze all my bras. Very high school, but very effective. "Kristy started a non-profit literacy program at the battered women's shelter," I explained to LeHump proudly. "It has a day care and she's helped hundreds of women get their GED and find jobs."

"God damn it!" Shoshanna shouted, diving for Kristy and bear hugging her for the second time in less than twenty minutes. "I am so fucking proud to call you my student! You are helping women help themselves. You are my hero!"

After a bunch of crying, pride on Shoshanna's part, joy on Kristy's and if I'm being totally honest...a little jealousy on mine, we all settled down and finished off the buffet of doughnuts, Wheat Thins and cheese. Shoshanna finally decided to hit the road, but not before we filled Kristy in on our project with Evangeline.

She screamed in horror upon hearing my plot and laughed so hard she had to run to the bathroom to pee. Maybe I really should consider a life of stand-up comedy. I could pack a house with urine and all kinds of other liquids expelled through the nose. As I daydreamed about being a famous comedienne and hanging out with Stephen Colbert, I idly wondered if Shoshanna would carry the baseball bat into her sister's house to get her money back. I didn't for a moment believe she'd use it, but she did have a bizarre flair for inappropriate drama.

"Rena, don't bother bringing your lunch on Monday. When I was on the crapper, Nancy called. She's going to stop by and bring us something to eat. She wants to make sure that we're alive."

That didn't sound good. The alive part or the Nancy lunch part. "Will it have Cream of Mushroom soup in it?"

"Definitely." Shoshanna grinned evilly as she walked to the door. "Just bring a couple of snacks!" She winked and left.

We sat in silence for two minutes and forty-seven seconds. Kristy in heaven and me in shock.

"I can't believe Professor Sue was in our house and she's proud of me."

"I can't believe she's a professor." I shook my head in disbelief and went scrounging for some chocolate. Nothing. I could find no chocolate. Damn.

I didn't need it after the carb fest I'd just indulged in, but I wanted it. My pre-menstrual voracious appetite was demanding it. "Don't we have some Reese's around here?"

"You ate them last night."

Dang it, she was right. If it wasn't so cold outside I'd walk to the corner and buy six of them. Occasionally the sub-zero temps were a blessing in disguise for my ass. I decided to go to bed before I ate something unforgivable. Plus, I couldn't handle any more weird.

"Are you going to go for Casssssanova?" Kristy grinned.

"No, but I may bring him a cassssserole," I giggled.

"I was thinking you might want to do some matrassss wrasssssling with him and his fine tushy."

"That sounds a little too sasssssssy for me," I laughed and punched her in the arm before we got so assed out, we couldn't stop.

"Why don't you ask him out?" she said, pulling her legs up underneath her on the couch.

"No, I've only seen his butt. That would make me shallow. Why don't you ask him out?" I cringed at the thought of the ass I considered mine, on my couch watching bad reality T.V. with my roommate. What in the hell was wrong with me? I needed to get laid in the worst way. Soon.

"Nope," Kristy said. "He's not my type, too built and too bad boy. Looks like a law breaker. He's totally your type. You are so going to drop your panties when you see the face."

I rolled my eyes. Hell, I was ready to drop my panties for the butt... "Don't think so. I don't need anyone else with a rap sheet, no matter how fine his buns are."

"I realize you've been traumatized by your questionable taste in men," she giggled, "but this guy is sexy."

"Whatever. Goodnight," I muttered, determined to get Mr. Wonder-Butt out of my head. "Oh yeah, what's Professor Sue's last name?"

"Lumpshclicterschmidt."

WTF? I almost choked on my own spit. Just when thought the weird had left the building... That was by far worse than my last name; it was the worst last name I'd ever heard in my life. No wonder she wwent by Professor Sue. I grinned as I thought up ways to use my new found info about LeHump to make our time together more fun. I truly hoped being armed with her last name would give me a little leverage in the 'you have to shave her bunions' department, but with LeHump, who knew?

I crawled into my bed fully clothed and shut my eyes. Are you there God? It's me, Rena... please let tomorrow be a little less eventful than today.

***

After the most bizarre Saturday of my life, Sunday was a breeze. Even brunch with my parents, Aunt Phyllis, my newly pregnant younger sister, the doctor, and her boring lawyer husband didn't faze me. Normally being within ten feet of my overachieving younger sibling made me want to slap her, but today she didn't bother me. Even the questions about my love life didn't make me want to chew glass and swallow it...because I lied.

Apparently I'm dating a really rockin' guy I met at the library on Thursday. Named...um, Jack.

"So what does he do?" Mom asked excitedly, separating her eggs from her bacon and hash-brown casserole. She can't stand it when her food touches.

"He's in, you know, like communications and stuff," I muttered, quickly shoving pancake into my mouth to avoid speech.

Why did I lie? It was so much harder to keep track of all the bullshit I kept spouting instead of sticking to the truth. My sister Jenny grinned evilly, enjoying my sudden discomfort. I grinned back enjoying her big butt and dark roots. Now that she was pregnant, she couldn't dye her hair. It pissed her off royally that I was a natural blonde and hers came from a bottle. I was sure I'd get karmic-ly kicked in the ass for taking pleasure in my sister's shortcomings, but aside from her wide ass which she inherited from Aunt Phyllis and skunky hair she was perfect. I was the fuck up, but at least I had a good rear end.

"How old is Jack the communicator and stuff?" she smirked.

"Thirty-fiveish. When's the baby due?" Maybe turning the tables back to her favorite subject...herself, would get her off my fictitious boyfriend Jack.

"October. Why didn't you invite him to brunch, Rena?"

I chewed a new wad of pancake I'd shoved in my mouth and stared at her. She hated that.

"Is his last name Snuffleupagus?"

God, she was a bitch. "As a matter of fact, it is," I bit out sarcastically, "and I didn't invite him because he's in Russia doing...um, work." Shit, shit, shit. Well, if that didn't sound like a big fat hairy lie, I didn't know what would.

"How exciting!" Aunt Phyllis gushed. "Does he have a T.V.?"

"Oh, Jesus," my dad mumbled. He had a fairly low tolerance for Aunt Phyllis's eccentricities. Jenny's husband Dirk ate and pretended he didn't know us.

"I don't know. I haven't been to his place yet," I murmured, praying this conversation would end.

"Well, if it turns out he owns one, have him come talk to me," she said.

Mom's brow furrowed with worry. "Phyllis, I don't want you sharing your crazy ideas about people in your T.V. with Rena's beaus. She has enough problems keeping a man without them knowing how crazy we are."

My mother and Aunt Phyllis took my single status personally. I'd sworn off dating for a while. I didn't understand why it was such a big deal. My Aunt Phyllis repeatedly told me she would still love me if I decided to be a lesbian. Sweet Baby Jesus, if it were only that easy. Hence the mythical boyfriend...Jack.

Being single in my family had gotten dangerous. I hadn't had a date in two months, unless you counted the hostile takeover of three hours of my life last weekend. I thought I was going to poker night at the church with my mother and Aunt Phyllis. They'd lied. It was a singles mixer for Lutherans who couldn't find dates without help from Jesus.

"Mom, don't worry about it. Jack likes insane people," I muttered, reassuringly patting my aunt's hand.

My sister laughed, so I leaned forward, ran my fingers along my natural blonde roots and started humming 'I Like Big Butts.'

"Mom, do you hear her?" Jenny hissed, pointing her butter knife at me.

"Rena, don't incite you sister. She's hormonal and she can't do anything about her hair stripe, so don't be mean."

Jenny turned a very unbecoming shade of purple. She gave me the finger, pulled her beret out of her purse and plopped it on her head, effectively covering her stripe. I had to think her bedside manner sucked. Dirk kept his head down and ate faster than I thought humanly possible.

"What about the aliens in my toaster?" Phyllis inquired as if she were speaking of something as mundane as the weather.

"For god's sake Phyllis, do you have Martians living in your toilet too?" Dad snapped.

"Yes, sometimes," she replied.

That was new. I wondered if the sock gremlins in her dryer would come up. Crazy didn't run in my family...it stopped and strolled and hung out. I was fairly sure it had taken up permanent residence at Aunt Phyllis's. I listened while everyone shot down all my poor Aunt's hypotheses and quietly made my escape before anyone remembered to interrogate me about my new love, Jack the Communicator, any further.

For purchase information, visit
robynpeterman.com/how-hard-can-it-be. ##

About Robyn Peterman

Robyn Peterman writes because the people inside her head won't leave her alone until she gives them life on paper.

Her addictions include laughing really hard with friends, shoes (the expensive kind), Target, Coke Zero Cherry with extra ice in a Styrofoam cup, bejeweled reading glasses, her kids, her super-hot hubby and collecting stray animals.

A former professional actress with Broadway, film and T.V. credits, she now lives in the South with her family and too many animals to count.

Writing gives her peace and makes her whole, plus having a job where you can work in your underpants works really well for her. You can leave Robyn a message via the Contact Page and she'll get back to you as soon as her bizarre life permits! She loves to hear from her fans!

Visit www.robynpeterman.com for more information.

Made in the USA
San Bernardino, CA
04 October 2015